ONE FOR THE ROCK

Kevin Major

The author thanks Anne for the nudge to start, Luke for endorsing the first draft, James for his fresh editorial insight, and the Breakwater team for guiding it to you.

BREAKWATER
P.O. Box 2188, St. John's, NL, Canada, A1C 6E6
WWW.BREAKWATERBOOKS.COM

A CIP CATALOGUE RECORD FOR THIS BOOK IS AVAILABLE FROM LIBRARY
AND ARCHIVES CANADA

COPYRIGHT ©2018 Kevin Major
ISBN 978-1-55081-687-7

Cover photograph by Kent Barrett

We acknowledge the support of the Canada Council for the Arts, which last year invested $153 million to bring the arts to Canadians throughout the country. We acknowledge the financial support of the Government of Canada and the Government of Newfoundland and Labrador through the Department of Tourism, Culture, Industry and Innovation for our publishing activities.

PRINTED AND BOUND IN CANADA.

 Canada Council   Conseil des A
for the Arts   du Canada   Canadä   Newfoundland Labrador

Breakwater Books is committed to choosing papers and materials for our books that help to protect our environment. To this end, this book is printed on a recycled paper that is certified by the Forest Stewardship Council®.

cheers, Donald

There's nothing funny about a slab of rock impacted two inches into the base of the skull. The obscene dent has sealed over, clogged by a clump of hair thickened with black blood.

'At that height you're talking a force of fifty Gs at least,' the pathologist tells me. 'Brain ricocheted inside the skull, blood vessels ripped, extensive intracranial bleeding. Swelling. One massive piece of head trauma.'

Otherwise the corpse looks in decent shape. There are no broken limbs twisted back on themselves, no facial bruising, no deformity of the hands. On a table nearby are bundled his hiking jacket and pants, as pristine as the day they came out of the shopping bag. Hiking boots barely grazed.

'Value Village will be tickled pink,' quips an orderly.

'Is that where it goes?'

'Depends on the next-of-kin. Relatives generally don't want anything to do with clothing. They could never wear it. They'll take the other personal effects, after the police are through with them.'

Which reminds me.

1

SEBASTIAN. SYNARD.

Doesn't exactly roll leisurely off the taste buds. A '60s
smell to the first name, and as for the snarl of the second, an
exiting girlfriend once told me it sounded like an ancient
Norse term for constipation. She obviously knew more about
the Sagas than I did.

Nothing I can do about the surname, but if there's a first
name in need of surgery, Sebastian would be it. Seb? No.
Sebby? No. Bastion? And, yes, you try growing up with a
name sounding close to *bastard*.

My very much in-wedlock parents named me after the
guy whose music was playing as they walked down the aisle.
Not Bach.

"Do You Believe in Magic?" The Lovin' Spoonful. John
Sebastian. Period after Sebastian.

Enough about my monikers. The addition of *Sergeant*
sometimes helped. Sergeant Sebastian Synard. Seriously.

Of course I was never in the military, or the police force.
It was Air Cadets. I was fifteen.

And from it came at least one tolerable nickname—
Sarge—fleeting though it was. It could almost have been short
for Sebastian.

She was sixteen. And a Warrant Officer. Two ranks above me. We got to know each other better at the squadron's annual Christmas party, 1980. Before the night was over I was calling her WO (as in *whoa*) and she was calling me Sarge. I loved her accent. She was born around the bay. I came in my uniform during a detour to a desolate baseball dugout while walking her home.

Explain that stain to your mother.

WO taught me a few lessons. Like go for it when you have the chance. Like life's a weird conundrum most of the time, so what's the sense of playing safe? Wind up fucked up if you have to. It might take a hell of a lot of finagling to get out, but you're a better man for it, Sarge.

That's me, for what it's worth. Sometimes I think, not a hell of a lot.

'Dad!' It's my twelve-year-old son, Nicholas. He has his own key. 'Dad!' he yells again, this time up the stairs.

I close the cover on my laptop and set it aside. Shit. Is it Friday already?

'Hey, pal.' I meet him at the bottom of the stairs and wrap him in a bear-hug. He's a good-looking kid. Smart as a friggin whip. Funny as hell when he wants to be.

I hold up the jacket he tossed in a corner on top of his back-pack. He lays his unopened iPad mini on the coffee table, takes the jacket and hangs it up in the porch. Why he doesn't hang it up at the same time he deposits his sneakers is not meant to be understood. I don't ask anymore.

'How's school?' He's in his first year at Brother Rice, a junior high a short walk away.

'The usual.'

'Exams coming up?'

No comment. He is already on the couch, iPad out, some too-violent game up on the screen.

'Should you be using your time up so quickly?' I have rules. One of which is a limit on his gaming. Two hours a day. With both his devices deposited in my hands at bedtime. When he is with his mother, no such rules exist.

He doesn't answer my question, merely shrugs and turns down the corners of his mouth.

'What'll we do this weekend?'

He shrugs again.

I deposit my hand on the cover of the iPad and attempt to close it.

'Daaad!' he whines.

'Nichooolas!' I grab him in a headlock, and start to rub the top of his head with my knuckles.

It's open season. He nails me in the gut with a fist. Hard. Jesus. Enough I have to let him go.

'Shit.' I'm bent over, half winded.

'Serves you right.'

'Shit,' I moan again. 'Are you working out?' It's meant to be a joke.

'Yes.'

'What?'

'I am. I'm working out. I spent my birthday money on weights and a bench. I can already bench press seventy-five pounds. Three reps.'

'Not at your age. You shouldn't be lifting weights at your age. It could stunt your growth.'

He laughs.

'I'm serious. Your bones are still growing. You could do them damage.'

He shrugs. It rots me when he does that.

'Your mother know about this?'

'Of course.'

'Whataya mean *of course*. Doesn't she know the difference?'

'What difference?'

I grab his iPad and Google 'what age to start bench pressing.' Livestrong.com comes up: *How Much Should a 13-Year-Old Boy Bench Press?*

'See,' he says. '*How much?*'

It shows up on the screen. 'Read it. Out loud.' He says nothing. 'I said read it. Out loud.'

'Cool it, man.'

'Don't shrug!'

He smiles. 'That kid doesn't look thirteen.'

'No, he looks twelve. Read it.'

'*A thirteen-year-old boy is too young to bench press...*'

'Keep going. Fourth sentence.'

'*Bench pressing can stunt the growth of young boys and can injure their bones, joints or muscles.*'

'Would you repeat that?'

'No.'

'Let me do it for you.' He hears it again, word for word.

'Didn't Lance Armstrong start Livestrong?'

'What's that got to do with it?'

'Didn't you say he was nothing but a bloody liar?'

When he's in bed I call his mother.

'Samantha.'

'Is something wrong?'

'Are you busy?' By *busy* I mean gainfully employed with Frederick. He's a cop and knows it. Enough said.

'No.'

'No?'

'Sebastian, what is it?'

'Are you allowing Nick to lift weights?'

'He's happy.'

'That's beside the point. Don't you know that the recommended age for boys to start bench pressing is fifteen?'

'He's careful. I trust him.'

'Trust has fuck all to do with it.'

She hangs up immediately. We have this agreement. I agreed not to swear when we talk on the phone. I redial her number. She lets it ring five times.

'Yes.'

'I'm sorry.'

'Good.'

'To get back to the point. Bench pressing could do Nicholas serious damage. It could interfere with the proper development of his muscles and bones. That's medical specialists talking, not me.'

'Truly?'

Yes, fucking truly. Not out loud.

'Yes.'

'Would you talk to him?'

'The equipment is in *your* house.'

'He would take it better coming from you. Man to man, you know.'

Do I detect sarcasm? Obviously.

'Do me a favour, Samantha. Have your boyfriend pack up the weights and the bench and store them out of sight.'

Frederick is built like an ox. He should be able to manage that much.

'Sebastian.'

'Yes.'

'Stay cool.'

Idiot.

I got that wrong. Very wrong. She's one of the most intelligent people I know. No, she's *the* most intelligent person I know.

Samantha, the love of my life (up to three years ago) has a PhD in Secondary Education. She was one of the first female high-school principals in the city. She's received the Prime Minister's Award for Teaching Excellence.

At university she was considered quite the catch, and I was the laddio to slip the ring on her finger. And I didn't have to work particularly hard to do it. As strange as it might sound, given the downward curve of the marriage, we were in love. Deeply and unreservedly in love.

We taught in the same high school for years. We built a spacious, handsome home. I became head of the Social Studies Department, while she became Vice-Principal and worked on her Masters by correspondence. We moved to Toronto for two years so she could do her PhD at OISE. In due course we had a child. We moved to St. John's so she could take a principal position. And gradually things began to fall apart.

It was a slow, bittersweet, steady decline. At its most critical moment—when it might have gone either way—she said it was because I couldn't take being stuck in the staffroom while she occupied the principal's office. We sheltered Nicholas from the worst of it. But he must have seen it coming. As I said, a very smart kid.

Then it happened. I blew up one day at a student who was being his asshole self once too often. I grabbed him by the t-shirt and yanked him out of his seat and shoved him out the classroom door. He fell hard against a locker. There was a time you could do that and get away with it. That time had long passed. It was immensely embarrassing to Samantha, of course, me having to go before a disciplinary hearing at the School Board Office.

That was April. At the end of the school year, I quit. Didn't take stress leave, which I could easily have done. I outright quit. Ten incessant years away from a pension. I would still qualify for a pension—severely reduced from what it would have been had I stuck it out—but a dozen years down the road, with no prospects of a job, certainly not one that paid anywhere near what I was making as a tenured teacher.

Samantha was not impressed, to put it mildly. That summer, two years ago, I weighed my options and Samantha weighed hers. When she returned to school in September, while I sat at home, read and drank Scotch, and continued in limbo, the skies became increasingly dark.

Then my father died suddenly of a heart attack. My mother had passed away three years earlier and dad held on in the family home in Gander even though he probably shouldn't have.

His house was sold, investments liquidated, bank deposits tallied and everything split by half. The old man had been keen with money all his life, and, unknown to us, had remained a client of a rather smart financial advisor. All told, I came away with several hundred thousand. Enough, it suddenly occurred to Samantha, that I could be living on my own and getting by even without a job.

So it was a stale smile and a nod, and out the front door. I picked up a decent two-bedroom on Military Road, but there's only me, and Nicholas sometimes.

Actually I am employed. Seasonally. Tourist seasonally. I've parlayed my teaching knowledge of Newfoundland into a business. I conduct small group tours of its outrageously colourful capital city. A combination of history, geography, and culture, wrapped around fine dining.

I call it *On the Rock(s)*. Works rather well, *n'est-ce pas?* Exotic, yet rough and ready. Manly, yet not without its seduction qualities. You see the rugged, scraggy isle of Newfoundland is euphemistically known as The Rock. And combined with the sophisticated allusion to spirits—although I prefer my Scotch without ice—it definitely has an allure.

Next week marks the start of the new season. Three and a half very full days. Six people signed up. (I limit it to six to add to the allure.) Fifteen hundred bucks each, all inclusive, except for the flights to get here and back. That's what I was doing before I called Samantha, fine tuning the schedule. And what I'm going back to now before crashing for the night.

On the way to my bedroom and laptop, I stop by the single spare room that Nicholas takes over when he visits. The bedside lamp is still on. Nicholas is sound asleep, a magazine splayed across his bare, pre-adolescent chest. Soon to be muscle-bound. Not likely.

I quietly lift the magazine away. What's this? *Dog Fancy*. I'm glad he's reading something, anything.

I set the magazine on the night table then tuck the bed clothes around him.

I stare at him and the rush of a father's love penetrates me to the core. I kiss his cheek and he doesn't stir, before taking another long moment of staring, then turning out the light and slipping out of the room.

2

I HAD A gutload of apprehension that *On the Rock(s)* could ever work. I went for therapy, cap in sweaty palm, to the provincial Department of Innovation, Business and Rural Development. They assured me I qualified. Then directed me to a small-business counselor. She looked very good in her scoop-neck white silk blouse and loosened black jacket, and liked the idea. A promising start.

Let's be fair. I had zero experience as an entrepreneur, though I got off on the sound of the word. I was forty-eight and rising. I was up against a wall and feeling the need for my self-image not to collapse in a heap on the rubble of recent *life choices*. I was also sexually undernourished. And Ms. Small Business was having her way with me, only partially tempered by the diamond-encrusted wedding ring on her finger.

'Are you interested in doing a six-week course?'

'What did you have in mind?'

'A trials-of-starting-a-small-business course.'

'Certainly. Would you be the instructor?'

'I'm afraid not. That's a different department.'

'That's too bad.' Perfectly acceptable language, though

perhaps my exaggerated hangdog look wasn't sufficiently disguised.

'Shall I sign you up?'

'Of course.'

And I was on my way. No good reason to draw out the inevitable departure and the devastation of knowing it was likely I'd never see her again.

Still, she did me loads of good. Boosted my confidence. And following the six weeks—business plan endorsed, start-up money set aside, adverts designed—I was good to go. As they say.

First season? Fall of last year. A little rough, but I broke even. Learned a lot, fine-tuned the business plan (i.e. reduced the level of fine dining, cut out the welcome fruit basket with the mickey of Scotch). I came away with a smile on my face and an eagerness to get down to business for season two.

Which is what I'm doing this early Saturday morning. Propped up in bed, laptop resting on a pillow. *Café con leche* on the bedside table. (Which I fell in love with in Barcelona several years ago, that and Gaudi. The man had incredible balls. To start that church I mean.)

The screen shows my list of participants, a full complement of six. Four women and two men. One a couple. Database showing name, present place of residence, age, food allergies, mobility issues.

Aiden McVickers, London, Ontario, 67, 'eats anything,' 'had a hip replacement six months ago, no issues.'

Maude McVickers, London, Ontario, 69, 'no allergies, but prefers the simple,' 'walks four kilometres a day.'

Lois Ann Miller, Red Deer, Alberta, 50+, 'no allergies that I am aware of,' 'recently climbed Kilimanjaro.'

Lula Jones, Jonesborough, Tennessee, 81, 'reduced salt, if on the menu,' 'has a cane, to satisfy the insurance folks.'

Renée Sipp, Riquewihr, France, 46, 'only to flaccid wines,' 'no mobile phone, no intention of getting one.'

Graham Lester, Toronto, Ontario, 75, 'nothing,' 'no.'

Photographs are not part of the profile sheet they fill out, but I have eagerly Googled each of their names, together with their hometowns. Fruitless except for a picture of someone named Lois Miller and a climbing party at the summit of Kilimanjaro. If it is Lois Ann, she looks exhausted.

Seems to be a relatively fervent lot overall. Ready, willing, and mostly able. This is the second time I've had someone from London on board. Word of mouth one likes to think. That or Londoners are in particular need of geographic stimulation. There's Lula from Tennessee. I know the type—eighty-one and weather-worn, but game to wrestle crocodiles. And Renée from Riquewihr. Sounds German to me. Sounds very promising to me. I like women without cellphones. And nondescript Graham from Toronto.

Let the adventure begin.

'Dad, you awake?'

'Hey, bud, what's up?'

'What time is it?'

'Two hairs pass the mole.'

He stares at me, his face wrinkled in incomprehension.

'My dad always said that to me when I was a kid.' Nick still doesn't get it. 'It's like Pop never wore a wristwatch for years, so he would look at his bare wrist and say…'

'Two hairs past the mole.' Nick shakes his head, grinning.

'It's almost nine.' I pat the other side of the bed, inviting him to join me.

'Gotta go for a piss.'

'I hate when you say it that way.'

'You?'

'It's so blatant.'

'Whaddya want me to say?'

'Leak is a good word. How about wizz? You know what my grandfather used to say?'

'What?'

'Make your water. He used to say, *young feller, don't forget to make your water before you goes to bed.*'

Nicholas laughs all the way to the can.

By the time he comes back I have a glass of orange juice set on the other night table.

'Thanks, Dad.' He takes a drink. 'Dad?'

'Yeah.'

'Ever think of getting a dog?'

'A dog?'

'You know, something to keep you company. Now that you don't have Mom.'

I forgive him. It takes a while. 'A dog? A friggin dog?'

'Shit.'

Now I've pissed him off and it's not nine o'clock yet.

'Sorry.'

Nothing.

'You want a dog. Not me. *You* want a dog.'

'Is that so bad?'

'What does your mother say?'

'There's no way. She says we can't leave a dog alone in the house all day.'

'You can't, Nick, that's cruel. And what about the days you have basketball after school. Would you give up basketball to come home and take Rover out so he can make his water?'

'You're not funny, Dad.'

'I'm realistic.'

'It wasn't my house I was thinking of. It was yours.'

'My house *is* your house.'

'Whatever.'

'Tell me what you mean.' My hand is in the air. 'And don't bloody. . .please don't shrug.'

So out it comes. What he wants is for me to get a dog, so he can play with it when he stays over.

'Nicholas, that doesn't make sense.'

'I'll come over after school for an hour every day. When I don't have basketball.'

'Your mother won't have it.'

'I can even come at lunchtime, cause I got forty minutes, and it only takes ten minutes to get here.'

'More in winter.'

'So.'

My hand is in the air again. 'Nicholas, pal, this is not good. Your dad doesn't need a dog. I got too much to handle as it is.'

'It doesn't have to be a big one.'

'Just a little shitter, making a mess of the place.'

'It doesn't have to be a puppy. It could be trained already.'

Why a dog? Why not the latest iPhone. That's what I'm thinking, and that's what kills me. Because I know how much I hate it when he plays video games all day, when what he should be doing is having fun with something real.

A boy and his dog.

'Did you have a dog when you were growing up?'

There's a gap of a few seconds. 'Bucky.'

He smiles at me.

I take him to Belbin's. I have a bunch of stuff to buy for tomorrow night. I'm having friends over for dinner. Two guys from university days, Todd (and his new wife, Jillian) and Jeremy, who's gay and whose partner died of cancer in January. Everyone knows I love to cook. Hate cleaning up, but love to cook.

Nicholas is not particularly thrilled but he doesn't complain. He pushes the cart and as I'm going through the produce section I tell him what to look for in a good carrot, a word or two about mushrooms.

'What's that?'

'Celery root.'

'Weird. I didn't know celery had roots.'

I would say there's a lot about food he'll never have a chance to learn, living with his mother. She was always good with the microwave. She likes a well-made, store-bought lasagna.

We leave Belbin's and go by Georgestown Bakery. I buy a couple of baguettes and a single *pain au chocolat*, which Nicholas devours before he reaches the car.

Only after several minutes does he realize we're not heading back home.

'Not Costco. I hate Costco. Every Saturday I'm with her she drags me there.'

Why am I not surprised? No doubt she spends her time in the freezer aisles.

'Not Costco.'

I drive past the turn-off to big-box-store heaven and head towards Torbay. But make a left at RCAF Road.

'Where is this?'

It doesn't take long to get there. I pull up in front of the building and turn to Nicholas.

'Just looking, remember. Just looking.'

'Holy shit.'

The S.P.C.A. animal shelter is no great size and has as many mutts as it can handle. Mostly big dogs, just one that could be considered small, and a few in between, from well behaved to mistreated, ugly to moderately attractive. Most of them prefer barking to looking like they'd want you to take them home.

The Siberian Husky/Border Collie cross is out. So is the

Siberian Husky/Shepherd cross, and the Siberian Husky/Labrador Retriever cross.

'Jeez, the Siberians really get around,' I whisper to Nick.

It's down immediately to the smaller one. She's a Chihuahua mix, (with what, no one seems to know). Three years old and named Cupcake. I try to picture her in the house. It's hard to do. I hate Chihuahuas, mixed or unmixed. They bark and they belong in designer purses on Hollywood Boulevard.

I can see, thankfully, that Nicholas is not enamoured either. A Chihuahua is not a boy's dog. Besides which, Nick immediately starts to sneeze when he picks up Cupcake. (Yes. There is still hope.)

'You're allergic?'

'Only to cats.'

'When did this happen?'

He starts to shrug and stops.

'If you're allergic to cats, then you're allergic to dogs, Nicholas.'

'I'll figure it out,' he says, eyes watering.

'No need. Your health comes first.'

He sets Cupcake down.

'How about fish?'

He snarls.

'Just kidding.'

We head back outside. No tears shed, which is good. The boy is coming around. Or, as I like to think, maturing.

A Subaru pulls into the parking lot and from it steps a middle-aged woman bearing a pooch in her arms. The dog is white, maybe twelve pounds, a bit of a puffball, but admittedly good-looking for a canine. The woman sets it down on the pavement, bound to her by a leather lead. Dog immediately rushes over to Nicholas, jumps up and starts to lick him.

'What's the dog's name?'

'Gaffer.'

What kind of name is that for a dog? Regardless, Gaffer looks to be a terrific shedder.

'What breed is it?'

'He's part poodle. Part maltese. He's a maltipoo.'

If it wasn't settled before, it is now. No son of mine is going to have a malti*poo*.

'Is he looking for a new owner?' Nick asks.

'He was my mother's dog. She's going into a home and she can't take him with her I'm afraid. She's heartbroken.'

'What do you think, Dad?'

'I'm sorry, son, as adorable as Gaffer is, your health is the priority.' I turn to the woman. 'He's allergic.'

The woman hesitates before responding, and is sorry, I know, that it can't work out. Such is life.

'But Gaffer doesn't shed. He's hypoallergenic.'

Hypofuckinallergenic. Dog breeders need their heads examined.

'All dogs must shed something.'

'It's okay, Gaffer. He'll come around.'

Gaffer jumps up on Nicholas, who's in the middle of the living-room floor in seventh heaven, having his face licked until he falls over backwards laughing like I haven't seen him do in months. The dog runs off to explore another part of the house, then rushes back to Nicholas and does it all over again. At least a half-dozen times.

I now have a dog. A dog that under no circumstances whatsoever will be referred to as a *maltipoo*.

The dinner goes well. Wild-mushroom soup for starters. Then roasted pork loin with Calvados sauce. The famous orange-almond cake for dessert. The meal is a hit. The dog a bigger hit.

'Take him upstairs, Nick. Take up his bowl, see if he'll eat his kibble.'

'He wants some of that leftover pork, that's what he wants.' The fastidious mutt has been sniffing around the table the whole meal.

Nicholas goes off with Gaffer under one arm, dog bowl in the other hand.

'Whatever you do, don't start feeding him human food,' Todd advises. 'He'll never go back to kibble.'

'Hear that, Nick?' I call out as he's halfway up the stairs. 'Kibble, no treats, nothing until he eats his kibble.'

The dog-and-boy sounds fade into the distance upstairs, only enough trailing down to confirm the pair are crazy about each other.

'He's lovin' it, Sebastian. You made the right move.'

I'd rather drink Scotch than go there. We sit back in the living room. 'Beverage, anyone?'

'And what's this?' Jeremy takes a long, admiring look at the new, unopened bottle that I set out on the coffee table.

'I bought it at the whisky show.'

'That was six months ago.'

'Saving it for the right occasion.' Actually I was saving it for the time I thought Jeremy would be over Devlin's death enough to enjoy it. He's having a rough go of it.

'Ardbeg Corryvreckan.' Which I take great pains to pronounce correctly.

I'm all over peaty malts. All over, as in eagerly setting out four Glencairn glasses and pouring a smart dram in each of them. 'Let's have a whiff.' No ice, no water.

Smoky as hell and the boys love it. Unfortunately it sets Jillian back a few notches. Her grimace tells the story, though she's determined not to give in.

'And on the palate, lads?…Sorry, Jillian.'
There's a pause while we savour.
'Exotic fruits,' says Todd. 'Fresh tar. Spiced peat. Loam.'
'Fermented peach fuzz. Pepper-infused Gitanes. Textured, very nicely textured,' adds Jeremy.

My turn. 'Definite creamed citrus. Unresolved sourness, but unresolved in a good way. Smoke—taut, muscular. What can I say but bloody remarkable.'

Jillian is left to shake her head. Samantha was the same way. She never quite got Scotch.

'Corry,' as we start to call it after several more drams, is a fine topper to the evening. And when the guests have gone, I put the cork stopper back in the bottle and carefully return it to what I lovingly refer to as my *beverage cabinet*. Jillian didn't get past half the first dram, and I'm not about to toss the liquid gold she's left in her glass down the kitchen sink. I pour it into a fresh glass, sit back in an armchair and reflect.

Life has its moments. Ardbeg is one of them. And Talisker, Lagavulin, Laphroaig, Caol Ila. The life list goes on.

It led me to start a whisky blog. 'The Passion Play,' Samantha used to call it, when things were at their worst. Don't get me started.

Actually, it's called *Distill My Reading Heart!* And, for those who get past the URL, it's not bad. Esoteric, but not bad. This is what I do. I match a whisky with a book I'm reading and banter cleverly about them both. Sometimes more than one book, but never more than one whisky. It's a pricey little pastime. And now that I have kibble denting the wallet, I'll have to cut back somewhere else. Underwear maybe.

Whisky is my one indulgence. Well, that and food.

It's Friday. No Nicholas this weekend, except for coming by to walk the dog. Day one of the new season of *On the Rock(s)*. Yesterday I left welcome letters and copies of the itinerary at the front desk of the downtown Delta Hotel where they are all staying. Our first meeting is set for 9 a.m. in the hotel lobby. New wind-and-waterproof jacket (bought online over the winter at an awesome discount). A very not-Tilley hat. Slick, slim, black leather, strap-over-the-shoulder organizer. I'm geared up and ready to roll. It's 8:50.

A *couple-most-eager*, as I have come to call them (I suspect it's always a couple), are sitting on one of the leather couches, each discreetly gripping a pair of not-yet-extended telescopic trekking poles.

'Aiden.'

'Sebastian.'

'Sebastian, Maude. London, Ontario.'

'Welcome, welcome.'

They seem a pleasant twosome. Smiling, if a tad anxious at first meeting. When they stand they look like they have been married a very long time.

Tilley Endurables has indeed been a favourite retailer. Matching olive waterproofs. The classic pants that zip off neatly at the lower thigh to become shorts. (I'm afraid they will go unzipped in Newfoundland in May.) And the hats, of course.

I noted Aiden rose from the couch rather nimbly despite a few extra pounds. Hip replacement must have gone well. Maude's four kilometres a day shows itself nicely. I'm always pleased when people don't try to pull a fast one on me with their client profiles.

Joining us after a very promising walk from the elevators at the far end of the lobby is Renée. Forty- six, as I recall, and looking not a day past thirty-something. Slim, dark hair, pale pink lipstick, intriguingly bright eyes. Noticeably fashionable in her European gear. An ill-fitting French handshake. She is, without doubt, more used to the double-cheek kiss. Very nice.

Attempt at conversation is interrupted first by Lula, looking very much the fit senior (despite the cane), though not so good at coordinating her outfit. And then Alberta's own Lois Ann, limber and efficient, if still a little done in by Kilimanjaro.

'And who are we missing?' A quick check in the slim black binder. Of course—

'nothing, no' Graham. Torontonians like to demonstrate their superior sense of timing by not being on time.

Graham approaches from the rear as we're all looking toward the elevators.

'Sorry, clan, I had to check with the concierge. I'm expecting a package.'

'Graham?'

'Absolutely.'

I sense something that will need adjusting. On my part, no doubt. The client is always allowed to be him or herself. Sebastian adapts.

I introduce Graham to the others, and in his own good time he slips his smart phone in a pocket of his red Arc'teryx. (Gotta love the apostrophe, even if I could never afford the jacket.)

I tend to think I'm semi-innately personable, and before we head through the sliding doors to catch a taxi van, I have charmed them through the schedule for the day, coloured with a few local colloquialisms and the promise of a stop for the island's very own 'iceberg beer' by the end of the afternoon.

'Newfoundland is very much an island, an open-armed island gateway to the rest of North America.' Given the opportunity, I do great tourist copy. We pass the impressive and grey St. Thomas' Church ('1836, the oldest in the city') and head up Signal Hill. Graham, who shares the middle seat with me, is seemingly too busy with his texting to notice. Live the moment, pal, you paid good money to do it.

'To the right—Deadman's Pond, believed to be bottom-less…until recent improvements in depth-sounding equipment.' Only Graham smiles. Surprise. So he's very good at multi-tasking. 'Above it—Gibbet Hill. Up to the early nineteenth century, criminals sentenced to death had their bodies hung there for public display and subsequent rotting. As we say in Newfoundland, enjoy the view while you got the chance.' Graham has the sole chuckle, without missing a thumb beat.

Signal Hill, the city's iconic landmark, offers stunning views of the city, its harbour, and the surrounding headlands. Beyond it is the open Atlantic. We begin on the boardwalk as I point out the most notable features of the city, answer their questions, insert choice local tidbits. 'There you see the Roman Catholic Basilica, consecrated in 1855, a remarkable structure for a city then populated by a mere 27,000 souls. The Archbishop of New York attended the ceremony and was so impressed that when he returned home he immediately set in place plans for the building of St. Patrick's Cathedral.'

'Behind us, of course, is Cabot Tower, most famous for being the site where Marconi received the first trans-Atlantic wireless message in 1901. As Graham will attest, he did a great service to humanity.' I couldn't help myself. Graham doesn't seem to mind. He grins as he continues texting.

'In this direction Cape Spear—most easterly point in the whole of North America. Sail due east, and you'll strike France. St. John's lies on the same latitude as Paris. On a clear day you can just make out the Eiffel Tower.'

'*Fantastique*,' injects Renée. It may be sarcasm, but I think not. Renée is easily amused when I include references to her homeland. Noted.

'And tucked in around this point of land—Cuckold's Cove.'

They're all ears. Graham pauses, mid-text.

'One of the many, shall we say, *interesting* place names in Newfoundland. Come by Chance, Spread Eagle, the infamous Dildo, and the aforementioned Cuckold's Cove being the most noteworthy. Iago to Othello: *That cuckold lives in bliss / Who certain of his fate loves not his wronger.*'

With the McVickers' trekking poles at full extension, we're off on our first proper hike of the tour. Only 1.7 kilometres, but spectacular in that it takes us from atop Signal Hill, down and around to its base, along the cliffside and into the charming old narrow streets of The Battery, once a fishing village, perched at the entrance to St. John's Harbour. Awesome views and, I tell them (on guard against being prematurely effusive), the chance of spotting an iceberg or whale. Highlight potential, definitely. I point out there's one short, narrow section of the trail where a thick chain embedded in the rockface serves as a handrail. 'A bit of a drop-of-no-return on the other side, but stick to the path and it's nothing dangerous. I've walked it dozens of times.'

Wind a bit cold and stiff, but hey, it's the North Atlantic. Newfoundland at the end of May. We don't breed sissies.

'We spent all that money on gear, folks; let's get some use out of it.' And off we go.

I take the lead, careful to see that the group stays reasonably close together. Behind me is Lois Ann, revived by the ocean breeze. She turns to inform those behind her, 'Of course, once you've climbed Kili, everything else is a cakewalk.'

Really? Kili? I've heard the climbers hire locals to cart their own personal Porta Potties up the mountain and back.

Aiden and Maude are too busy coordinating their pole action to pay Lois Ann much attention. Trekking downhill complicates matters.

Renée has just discovered that Lula speaks passable French (with a Southern drawl). The two have suddenly become kindred spirits of a sort, joined by a certain *je ne sais kwaw*.

And, surprise, surprise, Texter brings up the rear. To be fair, his device appears now to be in his Arc'teryx. For the moment at least. But no bets on how long the moment will last.

'Eyes peeled for icebergs and whales,' I call back to everyone. Always an uplift for those struggling with the steepness of the decline. There are wooden stairs with handrails in the steepest sections and they can see ahead that it will eventually level out, so no surge in the frustration levels of the Londoners. Hats off to Lula—eighty-one and negotiating boulders and loose rocks like a bobcat. She has Renée to offer a hand as needed. Lucky Lula.

It's impossible to provide any interpretation of the landscape surrounding the stouthearted six, preoccupied as they are by their footings and because of the gaps between us. That awaits a rest stop when we reach a level spot. As my mind tends to do when re-trekking familiar ground, it turns to thoughts of love.

In this case, to whisky. *Distill my Reading Heart!* Last night I scrutinized my beverage cabinet for the next offering.

Staring at me from around the corner of an innocent Bunnahabhain was a dog. A blended whisky named Scallywag, sketch of a fox terrier on the label. At the same time I was holding it in my hand, kibble-contrarian Gaffer came whining at my heels. My theory is the old lady who owned him fed him table scraps. The mutt has probably never experienced real dogfood in his life.

'No way, kiddo. Life's tough. And it just got tougher.' He stared at me, unimpressed.

So the whisky. What book to pair it with? I Googled *fox terrier, fiction*.

To make a long dog story short, Wikipedia has a section on film. Asta, wire-fox terrier, *The Thin Man*. Dashiell Hammett's *The Thin Man*. Master of the hard-boiled crime novel. In the novel, Asta is actually a schnauzer, but, fate playing into my hands, in MGM's stable of canine actors the fox terrier was top dog.

The Thin Man it will be.

Back to the moment. The stouthearted six plus one have arrived at a level spot halfway down the hill, no worse for wear. It couldn't have been good on the hip joints, but no one complains. In fact, smiles all around, and not yet a whale or iceberg in sight. The phone has even remained in the Arc'teryx. The leader is very pleased.

We look back up from where we have come and it is impressive. 'Well done!' I declare, at the risk of sounding age insensitive.

In the meantime, as we're standing more in the open, the wind off the ocean has suddenly become a concern, forcing the McVickers to brace themselves against each other and Lula to seek another hand from Renée. Graham and Lois Ann stand firmly alone.

'We are blessed, folks. You are experiencing the freshest air of any city in Canada. Enjoy it for a few seconds, take in the view, then let's move on.'

The McVickers forgo the vista, turn themselves in a clunky, graceless maneuver and head off, while Lula is determined to take a picture before she leaves. Her Nikon is entirely a challenge in this wind, but Renée holds her cane and grips Lula tightly as together they move closer to where the land drops off into the ocean.

'Careful, folks.' The wind is off the water so, if anything, they will be blown backwards, rather than forward over the edge. Nonetheless, insurance premiums leap to mind, and I take it as my duty to brace Renée who is bracing Lula, as an extra, man-size anchor.

'There now, folks, mission accomplished.' All three of us do a 180 before I let go. Lula fumbles the lens cap back in place, Renée hands her the cane, and they're off, back on track. As am I.

By this time Graham and Lois Ann are in pursuit of the McVickers. In fact, it looks like Lois Ann has jumped the queue and taken the lead. Energized by memories of Kili no doubt. 'Not too fast,' I shout up ahead. The wind does weird things to my words.

Once I see that Lula and Renée have a good handle on their mobility, I forge smartly past them, as the first move to regain the lead. Not to put too fine a point on it, but having Lois Ann set the pace could prove calamitous.

'Lois Ann,' I call. 'Slow and steady wins the race.' Perhaps she is in sudden need of a Porta Potti.

I approach Graham from the side. He is happy enough to be absorbed in the McVickers' stride. One eye on their heels, the other keeps checking his phone. What can I say? Nothing. I skirt past him, unnoticed.

That leaves the McVickers. Easier said than done. The path tucks in under the hill, for the final half-kilometre. At least we are out of the wind. But here there's a handrail and a series of steps, wide enough for anyone taking the trail in the opposite direction to pass, but full up with the McVickers, who insist on walking side-by-side, locked in their downward motion, step by infuriating step.

There's no choice but to dodge around them when finally there is a patch of grass to the side and enough space to attempt it.

'How's it going? Won't find this in London. Just look at that view.'

Straight ahead of us is the entrance to St. John's Harbour. The Narrows it's called. A channel opening out into the bowl of the centuries-old port.

'One of the best natural harbours in the world,' I manage to convey to the McVickers as I slip past with only a momentary stumble. They glance at me, unsmiling. They should be more impressed.

I spy Lois Ann several strides ahead. 'Hold up right there, will you please. Time for a *tête-à-tête*, Ms Miller.' I realize right away that practicing French was a mistake. The word gets mangled by my desperation. She is determined to forge ahead.

'Puffin! Puffin!' I yell.

It's like she's struck a brick wall. 'Where? Where?'

It's not the first time I've had to use this tactic, and it won't be the last. The thought of sighting the freakishly colourful little seabird causes her to backtrack immediately to where I'm standing, displaying an acute case of bird envy.

'Where? Where?' Zeiss binoculars at the ready.

I point to a spot of open ocean.

She does a slow, painful sweep with her binos.

'I don't see anything, Mr. Synard. Are you sure?'

'Reasonably.' I can't lie. 'They are pretty damn small.'

By this time the McVickers have joined us, with parasitic Graham a couple of steps behind. He almost collides with them when they stop. He looks up, and decides he can part company with his phone for the moment and slips it in his jacket pocket once more.

Lula and Renée bring up the rear, chattering away in French.

'Well, here we all are, *mes chers amis*. Out of the wind and snug against the cliff as we go past The Narrows and into the village of The Outer Battery to end our *petite expédition*. I peer ahead and something white catches my eye. Too good to be true!

'You should consider doing a bilingual tour, *Sébastien*,' says Renée. 'Your pronunciation is very good.'

I am tempted to throw her a kiss but think better of it. *Sébastien*. It sounds so much better.

I drag myself back to the moment. For it looks like I have a capital *T* treat for them all. End the hike with a bang and they'll forget anything negative they might have been storing up for TripAdvisor.

'Look ahead, everyone, and what do you see? Just tucked behind that first outcrop of rock.' They jostle for positions to get a better look. 'See it? A corner edge of something white. You won't see much of it until we get closer. What do you suppose it is?'

'An iceberg!'

'Yes indeed, a genuine North Atlantic, all-the-way-from-Greenland iceberg.'

'Hot dog!' exclaims Lula, who already has her lens cap off and her cane in motion.

Both my open palms are in the air. 'Warning! First, before we get there, we have to make our way past that narrow section I mentioned. Remember, glide your hand along the chain as if it were a handrail. Just stay on the path and there's no danger whatsoever. If you're not fond of heights, look straight ahead and whistle.'

Lois Ann is just about to make the grand maneuver to get ahead of me. Both my palms are in the air again. 'Follow me everyone. Single file. Go slow. Do as I do. Next stop—iceberg!'

And we're off—a jaunty crew, the smell of iceberg in the air. It has every possibility of being the highlight of the day, and beyond. There is that moment, that moment which stretches over and above the most anticipated, that causes a tour to reach a near transcendental state, a moment for which I have only one epithet— the *clincher*. As the tour leader you know you have touched each and every client so deeply they will never have second thoughts about what the tour is costing. For the leader, everything that comes after is tourist gravy.

As we approach the chain handrail, the path indeed narrows. There has always been the question as to why there is not a guardrail along the drop-off side. I sense the brain trust at Parks Canada has concluded there would be nothing suitable to anchor it to, and even if there were, there'd always be some damn fool leaning over it with so mega a camera lens he just might topple. Better that hikers grip the thick-linked chain and move along smartly, just as we all seem to be doing. I glance back to confirm it.

Barring any queasiness about heights, they are free to soak up the seascape. A few black-legged kittiwakes soar nearby, fortunately a common enough sight that Lois Ann doesn't panic. There's a good view of Fort Amherst on the opposite side of the harbour, with what remains of its WWII gun emplacements.

Once past the chained section, the path widens a bit, with the drop-off a near-comfortable half-metre away.

Suddenly, looking straight ahead, there's a jogger coming towards us. Sunglasses, black tights, and a hooded, lime-green jacket stretched on a tall stick frame. Clipping along with no intention of breaking stride. God forbid he should have to stop until we go by.

'Jogger alert! Heads up! Everyone freeze!'

He manages to weave nimbly past me, then the four-sticked McVickers. Where do these jerks get their genes?

The path broadens even more. The drop-off is more gradual and, in the worst places, wooden handrails bring an end to any sense of danger. That wasn't so bad. And the iceberg, grounded just beyond the outcrop of rock, is revealing itself nicely. The anticipation builds. The tourist synapses gear up, ready to ignite.

Although, when it finally comes in full view, it is, well, smallish.

'Isn't that what Newfoundlanders call a *bergy bit*?' says Maude.

Don't demean the iceberg. I hate it when clients swallow *The Dictionary of Newfoundland English* before they show up for the tour.

'I'd say there's a good twenty metres below the water.' I can be very good at making the most of minor setbacks.

'I doubt it,' says Aiden.

I have to admit it is a bit of a chunk.

'*Sébastien*?'

'Yes, Renée.' Thank God.

'*Sébastien*, is this a real iceberg? It's not like the pictures in the brochures.'

'You mean the Photoshopped pictures?'

Lula leans forward on her cane. I notice she hasn't bothered to take a picture yet. 'A Texas ice cube, you might say.'

'Let's proceed,' Lois Ann says. 'No mountain to be made out of this molehill.'

Smack me again why don't you.

'No harm done, Sebastian,' Aiden says. Condescending goat.

I'm smiling broadly. 'Yes, indeed. The historic village of The Battery just ahead. Fishermen were living here in the 1500s. Everyone ready to move on?'

But my instinctual headcount reveals not everyone is.

'Graham? Where's Graham?'

Shrugs all around. 'Perhaps he's ducked behind a rock to see a man about a dog,' says Aiden.

That dates you, Aiden. Time passes slowly in London, Ontario.

'Was he in front of anyone when we were walking along?'

Apparently not. Everyone agrees he was the last in line.

'When I gave the jogger a dart with my cane, I caught a glimpse of Graham behind me,' says Lula.

'She did, too,' adds Renée. 'Hit him with her cane, I mean.'

That would have been after we passed the section with the chain handrail. 'Anyone else see Graham?'

'Perhaps he went on ahead,' says Lois Ann, 'while we were looking at the quote unquote *iceberg.*'

Thank you Lois Ann. Discretion not being your forte.

'I'm sure I would have noticed. I was standing right in the path,' I tell them, smiling.

'In that case, *Sébastien,* you should go back. I say he is sitting on a rock, how you say, texing. *J'en mettrais ma main à couper.*'

Whatever else she said, she's probably right. Someone needs to go find the fellow. And that would be me.

'Please wait here. No one moves anywhere, until I get back. Agreed?'

Reluctantly, yes.

Okay, then. He can't be far. The path back is straight forward, to the point where two large boulders block the view beyond. The path twists in between the boulders, then turns to the left, momentarily out of my line of sight.

Eyes on the road, Sebastian. Past the two boulders, quick turn to the left. No more than twenty metres ahead I can see the end links of the chain railing embedded in the rock. An unobstructed view, except one section where the path curves around another boulder. Perhaps where our Mr. Lester has taken cover, deep into his device.

No such luck.

'Graham!' I call out, except there are no unexposed areas. Basically rock and scrub up a steep incline on one side and the drop-off into the ocean on the other, two metres of good path between.

No answer.

My eyes scour uphill, and I'm quickly certain he's not there. There's no way he could be climbing and not be seen.

'Graham Lester!' I shout ahead, in case for some reason he went back the way we came. He's dropped something, I'm thinking, and has gone back to look for it.

No answer.

I'm divided. Do I go after him, or do I go back to the others and brief them on the situation? It suddenly dawns on me that I have his cellphone number in my file. I do if he filled in the blank line on the profile sheet. I slip the organizer over my shoulder and unzip it quickly. With a tight grip on the pages I manage to work my way through them until I come to Graham's hasty scrawl. The number is there, and is perfectly readable. I say it aloud and continue saying it aloud until my phone is out of my pocket and the numbers punched in.

I brace myself, coughing to clear my voice. I will have to be firm to get the bugger back on schedule.

I can hear it ringing. Pause, ring, pause, ring, pause, ring. A few more and still nothing. I drop the phone from my ear. Useless. Even if he is texting he should have the common sense to answer his phone.

There's tinny music coming from somewhere. What is that? Someone's ringtone?

But there's no one on the path. The music isn't coming from behind or in front. It's from below. From somewhere over the edge, where the path drops away.

My phone goes to voice message, and the music below me stops.

Well, shit, if it isn't Graham's phone. I peer over the edge, and there it is, his white iPhone lying in a solitary, narrow tuft of grass a half-metre below, reachable if I were to very carefully kneel, bend cautiously lower, and stretch a hand. It's in rough grass holding to the base gravel of the path, grass that immediately gives way to open air, and a rocky, scrubby drop to a ledge and then straight down another twenty metres into the sea.

Jesus. The ledge hits me like a vicious smack in the face. The patch of red on the ledge.

'Graham!'

The patch of red perfectly outlining a head against a slab of rock.

3

BETWEEN THE BOULDERS comes the rush of the other five. None of them being careful enough. Nobody with a walking stick.

'What is it? What is it?' All five of them clinging together now.

One of my hands points to the scene below us. The other holds my cellphone to my ear.

'Oh, my God!'

9-1-1 answers. 'There's been an accident. The North Head Trail around Signal Hill. The Battery end. Yes. Yes. Not far from where the trail ends. A man fallen over the cliff. He appears to have landed on a ledge partway down. No sign of movement. I think his head struck a rock. No. I can't tell. It's impossible to reach him without the proper equipment. Yes. I'll stay here. Yes. Sebastian Synard. S-e-b-a-s-t-i-a-n. S-y-n-a-r-d.'

'My God. He wasn't looking where he was going,' says Lois Ann.

'He was always on that phone of his, head down,' says Aiden.

'Texing.' Yes, Renée, texting.

'What can we do to help him?' Lula demands.

'There's nothing we can do. It's too steep.'

'Then we pray,' says Lula. And in she pitches right away. 'Dear Lord, we pray for you to help our dear brother, Graham, in his hour of need. Hold him, Lord, until a rescue squad can come to his assistance. We pray, dear Lord, that the light of Your love finds its way into his soul. Amen.'

Amens all around. Including me.

As the minutes pass, our gathering enlarges on both sides, walkers and joggers filling up the path so no one can get through even if they wanted to.

It needs no explanation. Everyone can see the motionless body below.

Nobody thinks the chances of survival look good. Especially since there's a dark pool surrounding his head. I have to turn away.

Lois Ann motions with her binoculars to me and to the scene below. I take hold and take a deep breath, raising the binoculars to my eyes.

His face is directed to one side, his head in perfect alignment with his body. And, yes, that has to be blood across the rock, encompassing his head.

I return the binoculars to Lois Ann, who shares with each person in our group. And all I can think about is what I might have done to prevent it.

Renée, the dear woman, seems to know what is going through my mind. 'You bear no responsibility, *Sébastien*. You warned him of the dangers and he ignored you.'

She puts an encouraging hand on my shoulder. I wish I were in a frame of mind to appreciate it more.

The other four draw closer to us.

'What a terrible thing to happen,' I say. 'And on our very first day. We hardly knew him.'

'We hardly did,' says Aiden.

'Perhaps that was for the better,' adds the normally reticent wife.

'We all know what you mean.'

We do? Yes, perhaps we do. We have all been spared a deeper pain. If he had been a loved one, or even a friend, it would have been so much worse.

'Still, no one deserves such a fate. Life is cruel.'

'Yes, *Sébastien*, it is. Very cruel.' She squeezes me closer to her.

The other four nod.

Distant police sirens can be heard traversing the narrow streets of The Battery. Suddenly, the scene is all the more surreal. The sirens grow louder and louder, then suddenly stop completely.

I stare vacantly in the direction they will arrive. 'Stand back, everyone. Stand back. The police will be here any second.'

The crowd tightens as best it can, some people clambering up the hill to make room for the arrival of the Royal Newfoundland Constabulary. A pair of officers break through the gap between the boulders, one male, one female, both young, both fit, both prepared to take control.

'Sebastian Synard?'

'Yes.'

'We're responding to your 9-1-1 call,' says the female. 'I'm Officer McDonald and this is Officer Bates.'

I point to the body on the ledge below. 'He fell.' McDonald is on her phone immediately. I tell them his name, age, where he's from, why he was on the trail.

'We have an older male who appears to have fallen.' She takes another look over the edge. 'I would estimate twenty metres. He appears to be unconscious. We'll need the High

Angle Rescue Unit from the Fire Department to reach him. Do you copy? The High Angle Rescue Unit. Also alert the Coast Guard. Have them position a vessel in the water below the site. In the meantime we'll clear and secure the area. Call Parks Canada. Have them close the trail, and we need officers stationed at both ends.'

'Attention everyone! The trail is now closed. Please leave immediately unless you have information relevant to the fall. Members of the victim's tour group, please stand by. Everyone else, exit in the direction you were heading when you stopped. If you encounter anyone on the trail, inform them the RNC has closed the trail and they are to turn back immediately.'

The crowd disperses just as other police officers arrive. Two of them begin stretching yellow security tape around the perimeter. They have difficulty finding anything to fix it to, only low-growing shrubs and huge boulders.

It is not anything I could ever have imagined. We are a group of six bonded in tragedy. I have to admire how well they are holding up to the situation.

'Of course you will all get a full refund.' It is cold, callous, but all I can think to say.

'Not to worry, *Sébastien*. We will figure it out.'

It is another twenty minutes before the High Angle Rescuers arrive. By this time the scene is thick with cops. The rescuers have priority of course, and everyone else moves aside so they can do their job.

They are an amazingly well-oiled foursome, in helmets and neon-accented gear, draped with specialty equipment. The first job is for a medic to get to the casualty. A rock is identified to serve as an anchor for his rope, and very soon he is rappelling down the cliff. It takes him no more than five minutes to reach Graham.

We can see him bent over, doing what medics do, checking

the patient's vital signs, it would appear. The report coming from his radio is not good.

'The victim has no pulse. He is not breathing. He has suffered extensive head trauma. Severe blood loss.'

'CPR?'

'I'm afraid there's no point.'

'Are you declaring him deceased?'

'Affirmative.'

Our immediate response is to draw closer to each other, to experience the tragic news as one. There is no crying, no whimpering. We are there for each other, in the midst of our collective loss.

Lula intones, 'Let us call upon a Higher Being whose understanding of life's cruel twists are beyond our own.' Lula asks us all to join hands and bow our heads. 'Dear Lord, in your everlasting wisdom, let there be comfort. Please take your humbled servant, dear departed Graham, into your service. We pray, dear Lord, that the light of Your love finds its way into his soul. Amen.'

We are all there when the body is raised in an elaborate, bright-orange rescue stretcher, up and over the edge, from where he had descended so mercilessly. The body has been padded on both sides, with extra padding around the head. The back of the head appears to rest on a thick, blood-soaked wad of folded bandage.

His face, for all that has happened to his skull, is serene. His eyes are closed, the only incongruity is dried blood at the base of his ears and on both sides of his neck. His expression is one of peace. He could be merely asleep and dreaming everyone agrees.

'We were the two oldest in the group. The Lord chose to take him first. He had his three score and ten and then some,' Lula says. Her pragmatism is oddly comforting.

Four officers grip the stretcher as the ropes used to lift it are untied. They walk off with it in the direction of the Battery and its waiting ambulance, first having to do some nifty maneuvers to get it past the opening between the boulders. The High Angle Rescuers gather up their equipment, neatly and with admirable precision. Behind us, a police photographer is attempting to scale the hill to get some last shots.

Officers McDonald and Bates join our still-tight group of six, clipboards in hand. They need names and contact information, including all the data I have on the deceased.

'You're free to go. We suggest you return to your hotel. Give yourselves a couple of hours to recuperate. We would like to see you at Constabulary Headquarters at 2 this afternoon, at which time we will be requesting a statement from each member of the group. And if we feel we need to, we will also be asking each of you some questions.'

Everyone agrees, and with heavy hearts we traverse the short distance to bring us to the end of the trail and immediately into The Battery. In fact, public access is across the veranda of #45 Outer Battery Road, a private residence, and we have to wedge ourselves around a large neon-orange barrier that's been erected to indicate the trail is closed. A police officer stands guard, in conversation with an attendant from Parks Canada. They nod as we move past, seeming to know who we must be. The end of Battery Road is crowded with residents—solemn, wordless, except for a faint 'Sorry for your loss.' The word is out that Graham Lester is dead.

At the Delta they disperse to their separate rooms. I've suggested they call room service for lunch and have them put it on the bill. It's been a very long, emotionally draining morning. They all need the chance to come to terms with it.

I need a long, stiff drink of Corryvreckan.

I was expecting to be sitting with them all at Mallard Cottage with an order of pan-seared cod on the plate in front of me, a good pinot gris to the side. Instead, when I turn the key to the front door on Military Road I'm met with an excited dog and the memory of a near empty fridge.

'Dad, is that you? I was just about to walk Gaffer.'

I forgot Nick might be here. 'Hey, pal.'

He emerges from the kitchen, holding the last bit of a sandwich and a drink box, the lunch he brought with him. He looks at me, sensing everything is not as it should be.

I tell him the story, as much of it as he needs to know. The fact is I need time alone. 'You take Gaffer for a walk. I'm okay.'

He comes over and hugs me, and I really need that, too.

I don't savour the Scotch. I just drink it.

Later, when the dog has been walked and Nick is on his way back to school, there's a moment when I'm staring at Graham's client profile and realize I know nothing about this man. An address in Toronto. A telephone number. That's all. I'm feeling if I'd handled things differently he might still be alive. The police will have attempted to contact his next of kin. Somewhere, someone is in for very tragic news.

I'm just about to go into the kitchen to see what I can find for lunch, when a muffled ringtone goes off in the porch. The same ringtone. I had completely forgotten about his cellphone. I fish out the white iPhone from my jacket pocket to see who's phoning. The Royal Newfoundland Constabulary. The phone practically jumps out of my hand and back into the pocket. A hot commodity.

I intended to give it to the cops. Or did I? By rights they should have it, but I harbour a deep curiosity about who he was texting all that time and why it was so damned important that he got himself killed over it. I just want to know. And then maybe I wouldn't feel so guilty about what happened to him. I think I have a right to know. If the cops have it, I would never find out. They are under no obligation to reveal anything. A day or so, that's all I need, then maybe I'll toss it back over the cliff for them to find. It'll get to them somehow, eventually.

RNC Headquarters is at Fort Townshend, in the centre of St. John's, adjacent to what was once the site of fortifications built by the British to protect the city and their colonial interests. For a century, from the late 1700s, it housed Newfoundland's main garrison. It was a formidable, thick-walled, star-shaped structure, overlooking the city and all its vulnerable spots. It scared off both the French and the Americans. Except for the name and the plaques, all outward signs of Fort Townshend are long gone.

We arrive together in two taxis from the Delta where I met the others in the lobby at 1:45. They are re-groomed, calmer, and prepared to face again the events of the morning.

From reception we are directed to a small meeting room on the second floor and asked to wait there until the officer in charge arrives. It has a view of the city, although nothing compared to what I imagine Fort Townshend once had. At the window I am lost for a moment, disappointed that I will not be able to introduce the group to the charms of my home-town—its coloured rowhouses, infamous intersections, hidden alleys, its rapid-fire conversations, bustling food and drink scene.

'Good afternoon. Thank you all for coming. I'm Inspector Frederick Olsen and I've been placed in charge of the investigation of the death of Graham Lester.'

Jesus.

I turn away from the window. Facing me is none other than

my replacement in the life of my ex-wife. He is as stunned as I am to see him.

But he is able to stiffen to the task at hand. 'This gentleman I know.' He nods in my direction. 'Sebastian.'

As if he hasn't been screwing Samantha for six months, probably more for all I know.

'Officer Olsen. I hadn't realized you had advanced so far in the police force.'

He chooses to ignore my comment. He turns to the others and invites them to take a seat around the table which occupies the centre of the room. I assume the invitation includes me. Olsen takes to the head of the table, which has a large whiteboard behind it, and is joined by Officers McDonald and Bates, one to each side of him.

'I understand you are all part of a tour group. Is that correct?'

'Yes,' says Aiden. 'Sebastian's tour. On the Rocks.'

Olsen looks at me, with the faint trace of a smile. 'I see.'

Laugh, you fucker, and I'll maim you.

'And you were walking the North Head trail as part of your tour?'

'Yes, it was our very first activity.'

He goes on, question by question, to lay the groundwork for the meat of the meeting.

'There appears to be three possible causes for the fall of Mr. Lester and his subsequent death. A—he wandered off the trail and accidently slipped over the edge. B—he was pushed over the edge by someone who wished to injure him, and who may or may not have wished to cause his death.'

There is a sudden, scattered but collective intake of air.

'Oh, no,' says Lois Ann. 'That could never be. No one—'

Olsen's raised hand stops her in mid-sentence. 'And C—he intentionally caused his own death. In other words, suicide.'

The atmosphere in the room has suddenly changed. What everyone has been thinking was A has quickly turned sinister thanks to of the possibility of B or C.

'I don't mean to upset you more than you already are. And, believe me, I do realize how upset you must be, but the job of the police is to ascertain the facts, as much as humanly possible.'

Right. Anyone with half a brain can see that a seventy-five-year-old man on a narrow trail, constantly texting and not paying attention to where he was going, fell to his death by accident. Give me a freaking break, Olsen. Traumatize these people more than they already are.

'So what I wish to do, with the assistance of Officers McDonald and Bates, is conduct an interview with each of you. We wish to do that one person at a time, in a separate room. It should take no more than fifteen minutes of your time. We ask that the others remain in this room until you are called, and once all the interviews have been completed, I would like to speak to you all again as a group.'

What choice do they have? One at a time they leave for questioning, and return roughly fifteen minutes later. A least that much he got right.

He saves me until last.

'Please sit down, Sebastian.'

'Thank you, Mr. Olsen.'

'I've asked the two constables to leave. I realize this is somewhat awkward, but just think of it as a police investigation conducted by a stranger.'

I could be so lucky.

'Is there anything you can tell me about Graham Lester that you haven't already disclosed?'

'No.'

'It's pretty sparse, Sebastian. Is that normally all you know about a client?'

'I see them for three and a half days. They come, they go. They're paying me. There's nothing I need to know, except that they're not going to keel over dead because they have a heart condition.'

'A man *is* dead.'

'And he fell over a fucking cliff because he wasn't paying attention to where he was going. It doesn't take much to figure that one out, Mr. Olsen.'

Olsen leans back in his chair, his arms folded. His head a quarter inch from being shaved. His shirt tight in the places he wants it. An hour every day at the gym, courtesy of our tax dollars. A face that probably ambushed a thousand women.

'Are you through, Sebastian?'

I force my mouth closed, completely out of sync with what's going through my head.

'Every one of your group who has come in here has said Lester was wandering the path, using a white iPhone as he walked.'

'Exactly.'

'It was not in his clothes. We have sent a man up and down that cliff several times, had him search every square inch of the ledge. No iPhone.'

Here it gets dicey. 'Perhaps it flew past him and into the water. Ever think of that?'

'We have divers in the water as we speak.'

'Even if you do find it, that long in the water and it's useless.'

'At least it will confirm there was an iPhone.'

'You think we're all lying? Come off it, Olsen.'

He knows I'm right, the prick. So someone finds the bloody phone. What the hell does that prove? Nothing. I'm heating up. I have to be careful.

'It all adds up. Except for the phone.'

'Can I tell my clients they are not under investigation for murder?' The sarcasm unrestrained.

If it all sounds ridiculous, that's because it is.

'You're free to go.'

I get up from the chair and leave without another word. I return to the room where the rest of the group is waiting. I attempt a smile, but they can tell it didn't go well.

Olsen reenters the room, the junior rangers at his side.

'I want to thank you all for your cooperation. It has not been an easy day for you.'

No thanks to you, Olsen. I can think it, even if it frustrates the hell out of me not to say it.

'At this point we are operating under the assumption that Mr. Lester's death was an accident, that he most likely fell because he wasn't paying attention to where he was going. We haven't ruled out suicide, in part because we haven't yet been able to recover his phone. If we did find it, and, for example, we were to discover a suicide note, then that would change things considerably. For the time being, foul play seems highly unlikely. No one in this room is a suspect for any criminal activity. If we need to be in touch for further questioning we know where to reach you. You are all free to go and I do hope you are able to enjoy the remainder of your stay in our lovely city.'

Of course you do.

Outside I take a very deep breath. The six of us need to talk. I have my cell out to call a couple of cabs when I change my mind. I know a café nearby and suggest we all walk there. The walk will help us unwind and clear our heads.

The café is in what is called The Rooms. The outsized building has suddenly become the dominant landmark of the city, built, to great controversy, on grounds where Fort Townshend once stood. The Rooms is a combination Provincial Art Gallery, Museum, and Archives, its three sections echoing the architecture of the fishing *rooms* that were once so prominent around the island, where the great, historic business of the cod fishery was conducted.

The banter unfolds as we walk. The walk adds a piece of normalcy to the day, something everyone needs.

Before settling into the third-floor café we stop to take in the view. The Rooms overlooks the city from its central core and the sight that greets everyone from the outdoor viewing deck is impressive. A broad sweep of the old city streets, the harbour and the South Side Hills on its opposite side, all the way to Signal Hill in the distance.

All eyes are on it, the place that so quickly changed our lives.

'It's hard to think we were strolling innocently around that hill just a few hours ago,' says Lois Ann.

'What a difference a simple slip of the foot can make,' remarks Lula.

'Life,' says Renée, 'has, how you say, its pityfalls.'

'Pitfalls,' says Maude.

Even that has lost its humour.

'You are carrying a heavy burden, Sebastian,' Lois Ann says. 'And there's no need.'

Easier said than achieved.

Coffee turns into mostly morbid herbal tea. Lois Ann suggests passionflower. Knowledge of herbal tea is apparently a strong point of hers. Unfortunately, her first choice is not to be found in the café's wooden selection box which the waitress holds in front of us.

'In that case, chamomile.' She removes a packet from the box.

That they do have, and lemon balm, her number three.

I stick to coffee.

'A little George Dickel #12 wouldn't go astray,' says Lula, when her tea cup and pot of hot water arrive.

Except for me, her reference is lost on everyone.

'Sour mash whiskey, my friends, made in Cascade Holler.'

She means Hollow. 'Can't say I know it well, but I know it. I tasted it at last year's whisky show. Very nice.'

'Good man.'

Lula knows her southern whiskies and bourbons. The old gal's chatter about what she calls 'the little kicker of life' warms a heart (mine) in need of it. For the first time since it all happened, my head has moved to another space.

'What say after dinner we all go for a little somethin',' says Lula. Except she drawls it out to 'sum-thuuun.' You got to find humour in it.

'You must know *un petit bistrot, Sébastien.*' If it's a bar I do.

After a break at home to walk bowser, a light supper at Oliver's restaurant with the five of them, we're all off to Raymond's bar where I know we're sure to find something to satisfy everyone's taste. I know I need a Talisker. Lula gets her George Dickel #12. And as for the rest, everything from a Pink Lady to mineral water.

'So what happens now?' That's the inevitable question and it's better dealt with before anyone's reasoning power gets skewed by alcohol.

Lula takes a lingering taste of her #12. 'Seems to me the good ol' boys at the RNC are countin' on us stickin' around. Until they find that telephone.'

Lula is right. The #12 seems to be doing her good.

'In that case,' says Aiden. 'It's either A—the heck with the RNC and we all go home and Sebastian refunds our money. B—we all stay in Newfoundland and do our own thing and

Sebastian refunds our money. Or C—we continue the tour and make the most of it, and Sebastian gets to keep our money, which he needs and was counting on.'

What's with all this itemizing? 'Don't think of me. Think of yourselves.'

'You are so *galant*, *Sébastien*. So very *galant*.'

I could be blushing. It is hard to tell.

'A and B are fine by me,' I tell them. 'C seems pretty hard-hearted. Even disrespectful.'

'To be brutally honest,' says Aiden. And here he has everyone's undivided attention. 'None of us were close to him. Would he have wanted a bunch of strangers moping around, trying to act like they just lost a friend? I don't think so.'

'I can't see myself in mourning,' says Lois Ann, 'I need my exercise.'

Lula takes another drink. 'The Lord is not going to hold it against you, Sebastian.'

If I let myself be totally practical…I *was* counting on the money, especially now that I have another mouth to feed.

'A family that prays together, stays together. Sebastian needs us all.'

'*Exactement.*'

Tonight, with Gaffer walked and fed, he's now sitting pretty on the other side of the bed, where a woman and not a dog should be. His curly self is stretched out, head on his forepaws, the one eye that I can see keeping watch on me.

Dogs sleep a lot, but they know when they need to be awake.

'So, Gaffer, what do you think? Think I made the right decision?'

What do they say about people who talk to their dogs? I

wonder. Better yet, about people who seek their advice?

In one of my two latex-gloved hands is the white iPhone. I have been staring at it for ten minutes, debating the consequences of firing it up. More to the point, the consequences of keeping it out of the hands of the salivating lot at the RNC. Withholding evidence doesn't make for a pretty scenario. I imagine the dustup with Olsen should he ever find out.

Fuck Olsen.

Not a rational reaction. There's a pause, while Gaffer and I stare each other down. He doesn't blink.

Then again, when was I ever rational? And I'm not fucking well still in love with her. Let's get that much straight.

There's still something holding me back from switching on the phone. Fear of what I might find? I wouldn't be good with a suicide note, especially if it were something nasty. Like a tirade sent to an ex-wife. A parting message to a much-loved son. Especially if it's full of texting lingo and bad autocorrect.

Probably it's passcode protected. Most phones are. Some not. Anyone constantly on his phone might not want to go through the hassle of plugging in a passcode every time. Lester included, maybe.

If I did get in, I'll be a voyeur. A cyber creep. And say I do open the messages, read them, then leave the phone for the cops to find, would they be able to tell if the messages had been read by me? Probably the tech geniuses at the RNC could.

In the end, I fire up the little white frigger.

Bingo.

And this is what it gets me, starting 6:32 a.m. this morning:

6:32
-Awake. FFS what's his problem
-WAKE UP I DON'T PAY YOU TO SLEEP
-It's 5 am in Toronto

-Your problem WHAT'S HIS PROBLEM
-He wants out
-No f way
-Says he'll go to the cops if you stand in his way
-HA good one
-He knows it all
-His ass too
-Doesn't care take his chances plea bargain
-B shit!
-Gotta go piss
-You got two hands

There's a break of a few minutes. Must have been a long piss.

6:51
-Making coffee
-Waste my time
-Outa cream hate it black
Lippman says it ain't gonna work says scheme is flawed
Says cops got people digging up shit like this every day maybe he got a point
-F off it works in the states no f reason it can't work here
-Plus cops are keeping their eyes on you
-That was 5 years ago
-OPP got a long memory new name ain't gonna help

Lester ends it there. Another break. A longer one. Already I'm starting to sweat. There's a lot more to the guy than 'no nothing.'

I need a break myself. Gaffer follows me downstairs and into the kitchen. I can't handle coffee. I'll never sleep. I might not anyway. Lester had a scheme on the go. What exactly I might never know. Do I want to know? This is cop territory.

I'm at the kitchen table in the dark, what's left of the Corry in front of me. I draw up the blind and look out into the back yard. All's quiet on the home front. You'd like to think so.

I'm into the chocolate. Dark chocolate is good for the heart. Like red wine, only I prefer whisky.

My head is going nowhere fast.

8:05
-Anything new?
-Sun came up
-Did you see me smile NO
-I'm meeting him in an hour
-For what
-Breakfast
-F right off
-I'm trying to keep him talking
-I'm the one he needs to talk to
-He doesn't want to talk to you
-Tell him to text
-He doesn't text
-What is he a dinosaur
-Close
-Tell him to f call
-He won't
-Tell him to email
-Face to face his only way he's old school
-Tell him to F right off
-Relax take a deep breath how's newfie cold I bet
-Don't change the subject
-I'll keep him sidetracked til you get back
-How
-Trust me you enjoy yourself relax have a good time meet some women

-F off text me asa you meet him
-Not in front of him
-Figure it out

Right. Figure it out.

I could stop at this point. Power it down. Wipe it clean of fingerprints. Slip it in a padded envelope and drop it discretely in a mailbox, addressed to the RNC. No one the wiser.

If I weren't so curious I would. There's no way to get the F cat back in the bag.

The next lot begins not long after 9 am. He would have been in the cab on the way to Signal Hill, sitting with me in the backseat.

9:16

-Lippman's gone to the can you there?
-What's he saying
-Still rigid wants out thinks you're going to screw it up thinks all Mira can see is $$ says her timing is way off
-Leave Mira out of this I'm running the show
-Obviously he doesn't think so
-If know so Mira's in france and I'm keeping her there
-G2g
-Hope he pissed on his shoes get back to me asap I'm stuck in a cab with the dork who's running the tour
He thinks I'm laughing at his lame jokes I'm laughing at him

Guess who's lame now.

Why the hell do him the favour of reading any more? The bugger doesn't need me to feel sorry for him. He's pitiful enough as it is.

9:31
-Now he's gone out for a smoke
-Be quick
*-He's nervous I brought up about the money he promised last
week says he couldn't put his hands on it you believe that*
*-No f way he's loaded he sold that place on Jarvis call his bluff
and hurry up mad wind on top of this hill get this I'm standing
where Marconi stood dork's trying to make me the butt of his joke
f him*

Then the guy sends a picture of me and the rest of us, with
Cabot Tower in the background. As if he were a tour guide,
not an asshole.

9:40
*-Lippman knows I'm sending this text says to tell you another
10% or he's going to the cops*
-Tell him no f way
-I tried won't budge
-Tell him he's a f dildo

This break must be where he started down the trail. I
remember there was a long stretch where he wasn't using his
phone. Another where he kept checking it. Then this:

10:27
*-I'm back home Lippman's gone to his cabin in Muskoka a few
days in the woods*
*Might clear his head I offered him 5% he's not going anywhere
til you get back*
-Are you f nuts
-No
-I said the deal don't change were you f listening?

-You said no to 10 you're always good for 5
-Asshole!!
-Sorry
-Asshole!!
-Sorry
Lester you still there? Calm down you've always been good for 5
Lester?
Lost reception? Still in a dead zone?

That's it. Pinpoints the moment he fell. It pulls me back to the scene on the trail. The image of his head smashed on the rock.

Into it with the cops? I quickly Google *Graham Lester charged*. Scroll, scroll, nothing. Scroll, scroll, scroll, nothing. (Books of Graham Greene published by Lester & Orpen Dennys. Who knew?)

I go back to the phone and check for messages from days before. Nothing. If there were any, they were all wiped clean.

Still, seems to have been a shady character. Enough that someone would want to off him over the edge of a cliff?

Watch it, Synard, your imagination is taking you into dangerous territory. Cool it. Step back.

I look over at my canine companion. Gaffer is asleep. He should be sleeping on his orthopedic dog bed, but I haven't got the heart to wake him up.

I.e., Let sleeping dogs lie.

4

ON THE ROCK(S), minus one, has agreed to meet at 10. Shortly after 8, I get a call from the RNC. They want me to go to the morgue at the Health Sciences Centre and make a positive identification of the body. Olsen will meet me there. In the best interests of my stomach, I skip breakfast.

Gaffer, hungry and still in kibble denial, has no such qualms. I poach him an egg.

I'm out the door by 8:45. The bulk of what passes for rush-hour traffic has passed. The line-up to get into the main hospital parking lot is already painfully long so I duck into the parking garage opposite the spiffy new Medical School building, and access the morgue through it. As I discover later, Lester's body has become a bit of a *cause célèbre* for students. It's not often they get cases of such severe head trauma where the rest of the body is so intact.

Olsen and a pathologist are in the room waiting for me. I shake both their hands, out of the need to appear non-chalant about the whole business. I'm not keen on hospitals. I've never had reason to be inside a morgue. The wall of grey shelving filled with containers of body parts my stomach finds off-putting. What I take to be Lester is on a steel gurney, wrapped tightly in a white sheet. In another part of the room my eye catches the red Arc'teryx jacket, the top item on a neatly folded pile of clothes. It leans against his hiking boots, now permanently devoid of their owner.

'Not to worry, Sebastian. It won't take long. He's fresh out of the cooler.'

No stranger to morgues, the intrepid prick. He's enjoying this. He's getting off on seeing me whiten.

'It's an unpleasant formality, but the law requires it. Dr. Brennan will lead us through the procedure.'

The *procedure* is nothing more than unwrapping the head. Which is gut-stirring enough, thank you. A solitary extremity emerging from a cocoon of a thick white cotton sheet, looking like the head of some giant larva.

My experience with cadavers is non-existent.

It is definitely the head of Graham Lester. The back of which has been surrounded, thankfully, by a cushion of bandage. Someone has attempted to comb the rest of his hair and not done much of a job of it. The face, washed clean of any blood, though ashen and waxy, is that of the man I had laid eyes on for an hour the previous morning.

I nod.

'No doubt whatsoever?'

'No.'

'Perhaps we should uncover him a little more. Including his hands, if you would, Doctor.'

The doctor does, then excuses himself to speak to a nurse who stands at the entrance to the room.

It suddenly occurs to me that Olsen is doing this for no good reason, other than to subject me to the sight of the day-old dead body of a seventy-five-year-old man whose flesh was not particularly sightly when he was alive. Now that he is deceased it has sagged into grotesqueness, in no way helped by having been chilled. God forbid we should all come to this.

Olsen directs me to Lester's left hand.

'Do you notice anything peculiar?'

'Should I?'

'Look closer, just above the wrist.'

I had taken it to be some discolouration of dead flesh. On the wrist, where a watch would cover it, and about the size of a quarter, is a tattoo—loopy, calligraphic fonts entwined, shaped into a wrinkled circle.

'Two letters, a G and a C, agreed?'

I look closer still, against my will. On ancient, wrinkled, dead and waxy skin it is hard to tell.

'Possibly.'

'G for Graham, C for? You're sure his surname was Lester?'

'That's what he told me. That's what he wrote on the form. Why his initials? Perhaps he started out in life as a garbage collector?'

Olsen smiles, indulgently. 'Tattooing initials was common in the 1960s. Men didn't go in for butterflies.'

'Could have been a girlfriend.'

'Which one? Who's going to take the chance?'

Speaking from experience no doubt.

'So what are you saying, Mr. Olsen?'

'That maybe he changed his name.'

'Does he have a wife? Didn't you ask her?'

'Her name's Mira Campbell. Kept her own name when they married, or so she said.'

'Could have been a coincidence.'

'Or maybe she lied. Maybe she had reason to.'

'That's a lot of maybes. I thought cops didn't like maybes. In any case, the government of Ontario must keep a database of name changes.'

'It's a weekend. Offices are closed.'

I lower my eyes to the tattoo again.

'Maybe it's not a G.'

'What then?'

'Maybe it's a J. A stylized J. All those loops and curls.'

'J.C.?'

'*Jesus Christ Superstar*. My parents played that record constantly. *Hey JC, JC, won't you die for me?* Maybe he was a Jesus freak.'

It doesn't go over big, that last crack. His sense of humour is stuck in some rut.

Olsen walks with me to the front entrance of the building when we're finished. He leaves me with a veiled threat. 'Don't keep back anything you know, Sebastian, just because it might not be good for business.'

'Don't be ridiculous. It doesn't match the uniform.'

'We still haven't found the cellphone.'

'The guy walked over the cliff because he wasn't looking where he was going. Simple as that.'

'You're not a cop, Sebastian. You're an ex-teacher.' He walks away.

For the sake of the med school students walking past me I don't say what's in my mind. It's not pretty.

I arrive at the Delta at 9:50. Aiden and Maude are sitting in the lobby. No surprise there. The other three exit the elevator and we all merge into a team of six. Together we have experienced something horrendous and if there's a way to put it behind us, we must find that way. A unique bond has grown between us and with it we move forward.

Of course they want to know if there has been anything new about the accident.

'I have formally identified the body. The next-of-kin have

been notified.' Which is the reverse of what actually happened, although I won't tell them that, since I know now that being asked to go to the morgue was all a pretext. If I do say so myself, Olsen's little mind game got severely screwed.

'Is someone coming to collect the body?' asks Lois Ann.

'I assume so. His wife I would think.'

'Mira,' says Maude. Suddenly it's a surprise to herself, and her husband.

'Funny you would remember that,' says Aiden. 'When he was walking behind us on the trail we asked him if he was married. He told us her name. Mira. Or was it Myra?'

'Perhaps it was Myra,' says Maude. 'That wind made it so difficult to hear.'

True, yesterday's wind was a bugger. Fortunately, today the wind is not a problem. No wind, but no sun either. Newfoundland weather rarely gives you a double positive, but then again we don't live here for the weather.

One of the reasons we do live here is obvious twenty minutes later. We arrive in Quidi Vidi Village, another treasure within the city. It's a small harbour onto itself, an inlet just north of St. John's Harbour. Historically it was a fishing village, and there are still a few fishing sheds around The Gut, as the locals call the harbour, but today it is also home to The Plantation, our first stop. And to Quidi Vidi Brewery and Mallard Cottage.

The large yellow clapboarded building, fronting the harbour, is a *craft incubation centre*. Crafts people of various sorts are given space to work and to sell their wares. There's something about people working with their hands to make attractive, practical objects that does me good. There's a quiet saneness to it that generates a temporal shift in my head, draws me back to simpler times. For years, Samantha and I would give each other some handmade something-or-other for birthdays and Christmases. It was always special and we each took a long time to choose it. I miss that.

There must be a note of melancholy in my face, enough that Renée interrupts her walk about the various studios to sit next to me on the long wooden bench set in one corner.

'*C'est très difficile, Sébastien,*'

My high-school French reaps its rewards. '*Oui.*'

'I don't mean the accident. I mean you. You have a lot more on your mind.'

'True enough.'

'You have a wife?'

'Had a wife.'

'And she is no more.'

'Divorced. A year now.'

'It happens. Me, too. I was married to a wine grower.'

'I love wine.'

'I love wine. But not the wine grower.'

We smile at each other.

'How long ago?'

'For me—two years.'

I like this woman. A woman with a way to forget, to put it aside and get on with her life.

'Such a long way to come. Why Newfoundland?'

'I say to myself what place must be rugged, what place must be full of wind and waves? Where could I see whales? Where could I see icebergs? Where I can shop?' I Google all these words. What place comes up? St. John's, Newfoundland! Here I am.'

Good old Google.

'I've been to France. Twice.'

'With your ex-wife?'

I nod. 'I love your country.'

'You will have to come again. Alone.'

She stands up and resumes her walk about the studios. She has that unmistakable French feminine flair, her scarf arranged nonchalantly about her shoulders, her skirt clinging to her hips with such confidence. Her classic legs. Her perfectly unusual shoes. I see her talking to a potter, and then to a knitter. Before we leave The Plantation, she shows me what she has bought.

'A pair of mittens. For when I go cross-country skiing. They have one finger knitted, the rest the same as ordinary mittens.'

'They're called trigger mitts.'

'Trigger mitts?' Beautifully accented.

'In the old days, one finger to pull the trigger. For hunting.'

'My father, he hunts wild boar. Perhaps I give them to him.'

'Do you hunt, Renée?'

'Me? No. I don't like killing, *Sébastien*. That's man's work.'

I'm not a hunter. Oh, I've snared a few rabbits in my youth, but as for big game, I don't have it in me to pull the trigger. I would derive no satisfaction from seeing an animal slump to the ground and fight for its last breath. Not easy to admit in a province where every September men in their thousands, beer and rum crowding their pick-ups, make for the wilderness to bag a moose.

Still, the first thing that catches my eye on the menu, when we are settled in Mallard Cottage for lunch, is the Beef Tartare. Shameless hypocrite that I am. In the end, like the others, I choose fish. We can't go wrong with fish. So fresh it is likely still flapping about on the kitchen floor.

'Wine anyone? On me.' I pick up the food tab, as part of the package, but clients are responsible for their own alcohol. This will be an exception. We need the group bonding ritual of clinking glasses. 'Renée, you choose. You're the expert.'

'No, really.'

'A French woman from Alsace.'

She must, of course. In the end she chooses a Gewürz-traminer, pronouncing it beautifully. It wouldn't have been my choice. I generally find Gewürzt too sweet and aromatic for fish. I would have thought a dry Reisling. It turns out to be a Gewürztraminer *sec, proper, gracieux, et équilibré*, and yes, like Renée, easily embraced.

I propose a toast. 'To Graham. May he rest in peace.'

Simple. Unadorned. The sound of clinking glasses a confirmation that lives go on and we each make the most of our own.

The fish, in its various permutations—pan seared, skin on, cod cheeks, cod tongues, cod cakes—makes it easier to forget yesterday. The side dishes—braised cabbage, tomato coulis, celery gratin, kale two ways—refill our appreciation for our good fortunes.

Even Maude, who I recall *prefers the simple*, has been won over. You know it is a mark of success for the tour if you convert one mainlander to cod tongues. Maude devours several, and then takes the plunge into cod cheeks.

Her second glass of wine seems to have loosened her inhibitions. 'Sebastian, my dear, I loves the cheeky little devils.' She's trying hard to sound like a Newfoundlander. Her conversion knows no bounds.

'Maude,' her husband inserts, 'is a sponge for accents. Drop her anywhere and she's speaking like a native within hours.'

'It must have been the conversation we had with the woman who knit the mittens,' says Renée.

'Lord have mercy,' announces Lula, 'the woman needs a week in Tennessee. We'll have her tongue-tied and eatin' catfish and hushpuppies!'

'*Monsieur*, another bottle of Gewürztraminer, *s'il vous plait!*'

It is the first real laugh we've had together. How good. How not inappropriate.

A tour that laughs together solidifies. A motto of sorts for *On the Rock(s)*. It's all downhill for the rest of the day.

Next stop: Quidi Vidi Brewery. A two-minute walk. Tours of micro-breweries are becoming trendy, and my tour is nothing if not *with-it*. The folks showing us about are a chummy pair and we drift into the ambience rather quickly.

By the time we get to the end, and the beer sampling begins, we're a chirpy lot, eager to partake. A range of seven ales and lagers, including the famous iceberg beer in the blue bottle. Timing is everything.

The samples are small, of course, but given the wine intake at the previous location, the effect is, shall we say, significant.

'This refreshingly light lager is brewed with 25,000-year-old water harvested from Newfoundland's awe-inspiring icebergs,' says the guide with predetermined enthusiasm.

They seem to recall something less than awe-inspiring about an iceberg. The beer makes up for it. Drinking what pours from the blue bottle seems to tip the scale into silliness.

Aiden starts to croon: '*A turn to the right, a little white light / Will lead me to my Blue Heaven.*'

Harry Connick Jr. he's not. That doesn't seem to stop him. '*Just Maude and me, and Lula makes three / We're happy in my Blue Heaven.*'

He and Maude start to dance a little soft two-step. At which point I think it best if I call a cab and get folks back to their hotel before acute embarrassment sets in.

There is nothing more sobering for a tour director than having five mediocre-to-bad voices sing "Blue Moon of Kentucky" in a cab with windows wide open all the way down Duckworth Street at 4 o'clock on a Saturday afternoon in June.

'Hee-haw,' shouts Lula when it's finally over.

The cab pulls up in front of the hotel entrance, and I

manage to get in a few words before releasing them to the great indoors.

'Ladies and gentleman. We were going to take in an art exhibition on our way here, but I thought it best not to inflict ourselves on an unsuspecting gallery. Might I suggest coffee and a much-needed rest? We will reconvene in the lobby at 7 and make our way to a restaurant for the evening meal.'

Out they go. Cheerio and good-bye. Thank God.

'Military Road,' I tell the driver. 'The house with the bottle of Scotch waiting inside the door.'

Gaffer is at the door to greet me. The unconditional love of a dog—is there anything more welcome to a work-weary master?

'Come, Gaffer, come join me as I partake in the much anticipated dram.'

I see the light flashing on my answering machine. It can wait. I ease back in the leather La-Z-Boy, in sublime recline, dog curled warmly on my lap, the last enthusiastic dram of Ardbeg in the Glencairn glass. Sweet.

I would say twenty minutes past the last trickle of peat, well into a solid snooze, I hear a key turn in the front door. It can only be one person.

'Nick, what's up, pal?' I reposition the chair as if I weren't sleeping.

He strolls in. He knows he shouldn't be here. 'I was missing Gaffer.'

'Weren't you here during the day?'

'Yeah.'

'For how long?'

'I dunno. I came at 10 maybe. Mom picked me up around 2.'

'Four hours?'

'I took Gaffer to the park. We had loads of fun.'

'Does your mother know you're here?'

'No.'

'You better call her.'

'She won't mind.'

'I wouldn't be so sure.'

'I won't get in your way. I'll take Gaffer for another walk.'

'You're never in my way.'

The twelve-year-old is perched on my knees, Gaffer perched on his knees. 'You and me and the dog makes three.'

'Dad, can I come live with you?'

I'm not prepared for that one, though when I think about it, I should have been.

'Like, why only every second weekend?'

'That's the arrangement. . .'

'Like why couldn't it be Mom every second weekend and you the rest of the time? The opposite of what it is now.'

'You've grown up in that house. The judge thought—'

'I hate that house.'

'That's not true.'

'And there's no dog.'

Like I figured. 'Perhaps your mother will let Gaffer stay over with you sometimes.'

'She says no way.'

Like she would.

When Nicholas has left to take Gaffer for a walk in Bannerman Park, I call Samantha.

'About the dog.'

'What are you taking about, Sebastian? I can't talk to you now. I'm on the street, on the way to Sound.' Her hairdresser.

'Stop. Duck in someplace so we can talk.'

'I can't be late.'

'It's about your son.'

'I'll call you back.'

'He's here with me. In case you're wondering.' But she's already hung up.

I rest my case.

Of course I know it's only going to be the start of something much bigger. Gaffer, the mutt, has added a complication. I should have thought it through more. I should have known Nicholas wouldn't be content to have him part-time.

A half-hour later we are in the kitchen, standing by the stove, Gaffer at our feet, sniffing relentlessly. Nicholas is as happy as a friggin clam.

'So this is what you do,' he says. 'You fry the cut-up steak in a little olive oil, like we're doing, until it's cooked and all the fat is out of it. Too much fat is not good for dogs. It can lead to pancreatitis. Then we'll drain the meat on some paper towels, wipe out all the fat in the pan. Then put the meat back in the pan with some water and some cut-up vegetables, and cook it until it's done. Have you got any carrots and sweet potato? What have you got for greens?'

'Asparagus? Okra? Perhaps he would like a little cilantro sprinkled over top?'

'Dad.'

'He's a dog. He doesn't need to eat better than I do. Where did you come up with this?'

'I researched online. Holistic vets swear by it. They say it's better for your dog than kibble. As long as the diet is balanced.'

'Balanced.'

'All the necessary nutrients.'

'I know what balanced means. Nick, man, this is too much.'

'You want Gaffer to be healthy, don't you? It doesn't have to be expensive steak. Sometimes it could be chicken, or pork.

Just think how boring kibble is for dogs. Kibble, all the time, kibble. Bor-ing.'

'I don't have the time to be doing this.'

'We'll make a lot of it in one go. I'll help you. Then we'll freeze it in small batches.'

'You got this all figured out, haven't you?'

'It's fun.'

I can think of other things that are slightly more fun. If I'm honest, I like this, doing stuff with the kid. If it's not exactly fun, it is okay. Well, more than okay.

The doorbell rings. I'm thinking Samantha. Pissed off Samantha. I made Nick text her at the salon to let her know where he is.

It's not Samantha. It's the next person down the food chain.

'Olsen, what are you doing here? Did Samantha send you to pick him up? If she did you can forget about it.'

'What the hell are you talking about?'

So I got it wrong.

'I called you. I left a message on your machine. You didn't get back to me.'

He has my home number only. I wasn't about to leave him with my cell number.

'We need to talk. It's urgent. It's about the case.'

'The case? So it's a case now.'

'Where can we talk?'

'Do we have to, now?'

'Yes.'

'Coffee Matters.' I point down the street. 'I'll meet you there. In a couple of minutes.'

'Don't be long. I haven't got much time.' He's back on the sidewalk.

'Mr. Olsen.' He turns to look at me. 'A medium dark roast. Black with a single sugar.'

Not even a smile. Cops definitely need to lighten up.

I give Nick his instructions. He's to stay in the house with Gaffer. If his mother comes by, he's to do what she says. The stove gets turned off until I get back.

Coffee Matters is less crowded than usual, which means there are plenty of people there. Olsen has positioned us as far away from them as possible. My medium dark sits on the table.

'Let's get right to it. There's been developments. Significant developments. The Ontario Provincial Police did us a favour. They managed to get off-hours access to the name-change file. Turns out it was GC for good reason. Five years ago Graham Lester was Graham Campbell. The deceased, from what we've uncovered, had been up to no good. He was brought before the Ontario Securities Commission and charged with selling investments with inflated profit potential. A pure Ponzi scheme. Suckered in about fifty clients. Each one of them lost a bundle of money. But nothing came of it. It didn't go to court. The Commission fined him, but none of the clients got their money back.'

I am not surprised. For a very good reason that I can't tell Olsen. The white iPhone is flashing before my eyes, like a bloody lightbar on top of a cop car.

'There's more. We came up with the list of clients who claimed they lost money. Number twenty-two on the list—a Lois Miller of Red Deer, Alberta, to the tune of $550,000.'

I have to think about this.

'Her name is Lois Ann and Miller is a very common name.'

'No coincidence to my mind.'

'What are you saying? That she was out for revenge? After five years, she somehow found out that he had changed his name and somehow found out he was coming on this trip. And what? She signed up, too, so she could come along and push him over the cliff?'

'It's possible. A man is dead. As much of a prick as he might have been, he's still dead. It's my job to look at every possibility. There's a good chance it was an accident, but there's a good chance it wasn't.'

'Ms. Miller recently climbed Kilimanjaro.'

'I saw the picture.'

'That doesn't come cheap. Apparently, Ms. Miller drives a Mercedes. She doesn't sound like someone in need of money.'

'No one said she lost all her money. Sometimes the rich are the worst kind. They hate being tricked out of money, period.'

'Speculation.'

'What was the name of the person in the picture, on the summit of Kilimanjaro?'

I don't need to be reminded.

'So, say she somehow got to him, *when the five other people who were around didn't notice…*'

'You were all preoccupied with an iceberg, or what you tried to pass off as one.'

'Fuck it, Olsen, take her in, charge her. If you're so bloody sure.'

I sit back in the chair before someone in the coffee shop gets wind of the hostility. There's a cooling off when neither of us says anything.

Then he comes out with it. 'I need you.'

'How lovely. Need my advice on how to get it up?'

'Listen, Synard, this has turned into a murder investigation. You got that?'

Eventually I give him the satisfaction of a shrug.

'You're in a unique position to find out a lot more than we already know. If I take her in for questioning, she'll clam up. The cover is completely shot.'

'Do I get a badge?'

'You get the satisfaction of helping to put someone behind

bars who killed a man.'

'*If* she killed a man.'

'If.'

Another pause.

'What do you want me to do?'

'How much longer do you have with this crowd?'

'The tour ends Monday afternoon. They all fly out that evening.'

'You can find out a lot in a day and a half.'

'When do you see them again?'

'Shit.' I grab a quick look at my phone. 'In half an hour. We're having dinner together at The Fish Exchange.'

'Good. So, relax, act as if nothing has changed since you last saw them. You had a rest. You watched a little television. You read a book. I follow your blog, by the way. Do you get many hits?'

'Enough that I don't need yours.'

Now he smiles. 'That, you have no control over.' A second prickish smile. 'Obviously, as far as they know, we haven't met. If they ask whether the police have been in touch, tell them the investigation has just about wrapped up. As soon as the body is flown out, that will be the end of it.'

'What else?'

'Play it cool. Ask a few personal questions maybe. Just be careful. It can't be obvious you're fishing for anything. Take tonight to see how it goes. Give me a call when you get home.' He takes out his card. 'From now on don't call me at the station.' He writes his cell number on the back.

I don't return the favour.

Outside the coffee shop, I look up the street and see Samantha's car parked outside the house. That's the last thing I need. Olsen must notice it, too, but doesn't say anything. He walks past the house and stops in front of an unmarked car.

'Wait in the car,' I tell him. 'Give me a minute.'

Inside the house there is a mother-son argument in full flight. I walk past Samantha, who at least had the courtesy to stay in the porch. I run up the stairs, then back down a few seconds later. Samantha and I have not exchanged a word.

When I reach Olsen's car, he rolls down the window.

'I got something for you. I found it. It needs to be recharged.'

I hand him the iPhone. Is he surprised?

No.

I'm tempted to walk past the house and back to the coffee shop until everything cools by about thirty decibels. It would probably be seen as taking sides. No matter what I do, I can't win.

'Hi, everyone. It's only me, the owner and chief resident. Don't let me be the one to interrupt the fireworks. Please continue.'

'Sebastian, grow up, for God's sake.'

That's refreshing. My hands are in the air. I am not about to go there. I walk past her and into the living room.

'Did you give him permission to come here?'

'As a matter of fact, no. He walked here on his own.'

'To play with the goddamn dog, he said. Did you put him up to this?'

'I didn't put him up to anything. The last time I checked he had a mind of his own.'

'He's spending too much time here. It's not in the agreement.'

'He enjoys the company.'

'Did you get him a dog so this would happen? I wouldn't put it past you.'

'I got a dog because I happen to like dogs.'

'Bullshit.'

'Let me rephrase that. *We* got a dog, because we both happen to like dogs. And since said dog is not occupying any of your personal space, you have no input on the question of whether Gaffer should have come into this house.'

Gaffer is cowering on the couch, Nicholas beside him, running his hand through his coat.

'It's time to go, Nick.'

'I don't want to.'

'I'm sorry, pal. I have to be somewhere. I have people waiting for me.'

'I haven't finishing making his food.'

'I'll finish it when I come home.'

Reluctantly he stands up and moves towards the porch, trying to ignore his mother who is filling up most of the space.

'See you, Nick. Gaffer says good-bye.'

'See you, Gaffer.' No word to me as he goes out the door.

Which leaves the final word to Samantha. 'See what you've done, Sebastian. You've made everything worse.'

Like I said, I can't win.

I'm to meet everyone at 6:45 in the lobby. It's already 6:55 when I get to the Delta. I've had no time to get my head around this.

'Sorry, I'm late. Everyone ready to go?'

'Aye, laddie,' says Aiden.

Not a good sign. 'Everyone had a rest?'

Yes, they all agree, it was good to have a worry-free couple of hours. Booze-free as well I would hope, but don't ask.

'And you, Sebastian, did you manage to have a wee nap?'

What's with the Scottish?

'Or did you have a wee dram instead?' They all smile.

'We discovered your whisky blog!'

In French, '*Distill mon coeur de lecture!*'

'Aye,' says Lula. Leading to ayes all around.

They won't take no for an answer. While we're sipping prosecco and waiting for the appetizers at The Fish Exchange, I give them the lowdown on the blog.

'Do you get many…what do you call them, you know, when people look at what you wrote.'

'Hits,' says Lois Ann. 'Do you get many hits?'

'Enough to keep me doing it.'

'What's the most you got in one day?'

'I don't really know.' I do know. Thirty-six. Pathetic.

'Do you spend much time on the Internet, Lois?'

'Too much.' Her answer comes right away. She apparently doesn't mind that I dropped her second name. Okay, that's a start.

'Facebook?' says Lula, hoping to sound cool.

'Waste of time. Not for me,' says Lois Ann. 'I check stock prices. Keep track of the markets. Check out travel sites.'

'Where are you going next?' asks Aiden.

'Next month I'm taking a cruise into the Northwest Passage.'

That doesn't come cheap.

'Sounds cold.'

'I'm not good in heat.'

I would tend to think so. Lois Ann does have a certain glacial quality about her.

'The Northwest Passage has been on my bucket list for years,' she adds.

'Oh, I hate that term,' says Maude.

'When you get to be my age,' says Lula, 'your bucket is definitely listing!'

'Aye!' Followed by a muted jolliness all around.

I have to steer the conversation back to Lois Ann. In the meantime the appetizers arrive. I had pointed them towards something on the menu, its name serving my purpose. An appetizer called Bang Bang Shrimp. We ordered a few portions that we now divvy among us. In terms of the level of enthusiasm for the group choice, Lois Ann ranks at the bottom. Interesting.

I tread boldly, but casually. I ease into the topic of revenge killing, taking a well-disguised, circuitous route.

'Who here remembers Bo Derek?'

'*10!*' exclaims Aiden. 'She was a definite 10 in my books.'

Maude looks at him sideways. 'I used to love Ravel's *Boléro*. Until that movie came along.' Speaking of a glacial quality...'

'Well,' I explain, 'before *10* there was *Orca: The Killer Whale*, filmed right here in Newfoundland, with Bo Derek as Annie, legless in Petty Harbour due to a nasty bite by said whale.'

'Really?'

'Indeed. The orca had been wronged and was seeking revenge.'

My eyes sweep by Lois Ann. I do detect unease. Another point for Olsen.

I quickly decide to make one more casual thrust. 'It's not called a killer whale for nothing.'

Here is where things really get interesting. Lois Ann takes a curled-up shrimp and sinks it into some red chili sauce. It hangs dripping over her plate until she draws it whole into her mouth, in one slick, premeditated motion.

What exactly to make of that I'm not sure. But I figure I better get out before she starts suspecting something.

I quickly move us right along. 'Forecast for tomorrow looks good.' In Newfoundland, conversation about the weather is the great equalizer. Any two people meet and the weather is the first thing they talk about. We get so much of it, of all kinds, sometimes in the same day.

The change of topic seems to have calmed Lois Ann. She sets her plate aside, having done with the seafood.

'In which case we'll start the morning by taking the walking trail through the city as planned.'

'Wonderful, *Sébastien*. I always like a walk in the morning. Something to stir the blood. I always feel better when I'm in motion.'

I won't let my mind go there. Renée is such a delicious contrast.

Right on cue, the entrées arrive. It's always so much easier when clients love to eat. It goes a long way in the bonding process.

I feel myself loosening up. 'You crowd all love a good scoff.'

'Scoff, *Sébastien*? Newfoundlanders can sound so naughty.'

And where do I go with this? Is she flirting with me, or has the word just been lost in translation?

'A scoff,' Maude repeats. 'A meal.'

'A feed,' says Aiden. 'A blowout.'

'Ah,' says Renée, '*Mangez bien, riez souvent, aimez beaucoup!*'

What it means I don't exactly know. Eat, drink, and be merry? I have a feeling it's more than just merry.

Lula adds her bit. 'I just had a hankering for cornbread was all.'

The banter is driving Lois Ann crazy. 'Okay,' she says. 'We get the point. Let's move on, shall we?'

The condescension in her voice doesn't go over well with the others. It's my first indication of any personality clashes within the group.

In fact we do move on. I suggest we walk to a nearby café for coffee and dessert. A chance for Lois Ann to cool her heels.

Once we get there, however, the chatter fires up, as strong as ever. By the time dessert arrives we've run the gamut from music to movies to *The Dictionary of Newfoundland English*. The last prompted by one of the choices on the dessert menu—fried toutens, with maple syrup, stewed apples, cinnamon sugar, vanilla bean ice cream, and candied pecans.

'Darn tootin, I'll have a touten,' says Lula. 'What the heck is a *touten*?'

'Touten is basically fried bread dough,' I explain, 'traditionally served with molasses, but here spruced up a bit.'

'Not to be confused with *damper dog* and *bangbelly*,' Maude inserts.

Really, Maude? They know this in London, Ontario?

Aiden jumps in. 'We bought a copy of *The Dictionary of Newfoundland English* before we came. She read it through.'

Several times, by the sound of it.

'Maude was a librarian,' Aiden adds. 'She has a thing for dictionaries.'

And a thing for toutens, by the way she devours hers when it arrives. I notice her scraping away the toppings to get to the bare essence of the touten. Renée, on the other hand, seems to savour the mixture of tastes.

'There's only one thing I would change,' she says. 'Instead of ice cream, I would have preferred whipped cream. Whipped cream infused with whisky, a dollop on your touten—what do you think, *Sébastien*? Succulent, *n'est-ce pas*?'

Indeed.

It makes for a tough slog to the end of the dessert. When the group parts company back at the Delta a short while later, all I can think of, as Rénee walks gainfully down the corridor and into the elevator, is the likelihood of whipped cream.

It is an hour later before I get around to calling Olsen. First I take a shower, a cold one, figuratively speaking. Then I walk the dog. But this time my body and mind are clear enough that I figure I can deal with Olsen and whatever the delivery of the iPhone has prompted.

I dial his number. He's not answering. A few minutes later he calls back.

'So you're alone now.'

'I was in the shower.'

I won't ask where.

'What did you find out?' he says.

I give him the lowdown on the meal. The threads of conversation, the reaction of Lois (Ann). He seems to be digesting them as I speak, his verbal reactions amounting to the occasional grunt of approval. He's likely writing notes.

'What do you think?'

'That she's hiding something.'

'I think you're probably right.' He deserves to be right, some of the time.

'There's nothing concrete,' he says, 'but all this is useful. It's helping to shape a profile. We found out a few other things. Things you should know. She's licensed to carry a firearm.'

Really? Right away I make the link. 'Bang Bang Shrimp. Get it?'

Olsen doesn't respond. The bugger is smiling no doubt, indulgently.

'A rifle, strictly for hunting purposes, of course. Two elk to date. Two white-tailed deer. Allocation for a moose, but no luck.'

'I'll remember to keep my antlers at home.'

'She has a license to operate heavy equipment.'

'Those bloody big trucks, like you see in pictures of the Tar Sands?'

'Could be. We don't know where she worked, just that she has the license.'

'So she's an elk-huntin, truck-drivin…'

'There's more. She used to live in Calgary, married to a high-profile criminal lawyer—Travis Miller. They divorced seven years ago, but she kept his name. She ended up with a very big settlement. Two million big.'

'So she could afford to lose a few hundred thousand.'

'That's still a good chunk of change.'

'Good enough to make her kill someone?'

'That's still the question.'

'Does that mean I remain at my post, Inspector?'

'If you're still up for it?'

'Absolutely. I don't know about you, but getting up for it has never been a problem.'

I enjoy the humourless pause.

'It's what you do with it when you're up.' He coughs, the ass. 'Are you prepared to carry on as you planned? See where it takes us.'

'That's it?'

'What you've found out is very useful. Hopefully, there's more. Call me at any time.'

A full-on pause.

'There is the matter of the iPhone,' he says.

'Right. So there is. Interesting, wasn't it?'

'You could be charged with withholding evidence.'

'Not when I'm on the payroll, so to speak.'

There's a few seconds, again. 'The OPP have a search on for this guy Lippman.'

'What about the wife?'

'She's in Europe. Apparently arriving back in Canada tomorrow. The son is on his way here to accompany the body back to Toronto.'

That's the end of the conversation, for now. As he would have it, the investigation continues.

'Good night.'

'Good night.' Whatever that implies.

I pour myself a good shot of Scallywag, the dram of the month, and set it on the end table. I toss *The Thin Man* down beside it. Upstairs, I change into pajamas, before returning and settling into the chair. It's close to midnight and I need unwinding.

Sebastian Synard—disgraced ex-teacher turned tour guide, turned operative for the Royal Newfoundland Constabulary. A little trumpet fanfare, muted.

Across the room, the mutt, curled in a corner of the couch, is looking back at me. 'So, Gaffer, here we are.'

Gaffer runs across the room and makes a leap into my lap, one paw nipping the privates.

'Ahhh, Gaffer, man, I love you, too.' He curls himself into a ball on my lap.

He sniffs the air. He seems to approve of what sits in the glass. Good dog.

I read *The Maltese Falcon* years ago, and the book open in front of me is told in the same curt, no nonsense style. It's what I need.

I get through fifty pages then wake up two hours later, the book on my chest, my neck in a slump against the back of the chair. I straighten it, wincing with pain. Gaffer hasn't moved. He reminds me of the mutt in the book.

I'm feeling an affinity with Nick Charles, Hammett's private eye, although I'd like to think I'd have a bit more class around booze. He drinks at the drop of a hat. He's droll. I like droll. There's not enough droll people in the world, I'm thinking as I climb the stairs, Gaffer at my heels.

Day Three. The last full day with The Newfoundland Expedition Force. We have an itinerary, now a modified itinerary.

'Just a little change in plans, folks. We'll head to the Provincial Museum at The Rooms this morning, instead of tomorrow morning, and the visit to the Fluvarium planned for this morning we'll take in tomorrow.'

We're standing together in our usual spot in the lobby of the Delta. No one finds reason to complain, a good sign that any slight rifts between them have healed overnight.

'You're our fearless leader, Sebastian,' says Aiden. Facetiousness is not his strong suit.

'We are in your hands, *Sébastien.*'

Thank you, Renée. I'll keep that image in my mind all day.

'Let's hoof it,' says Lula, her cane already in motion.

Little does she know.

We board a taxi van and we're off to The Rooms.

Much of the museum's second floor focuses on the province's natural history. Immediately the casual visitor stands within spitting distance of *Rangifer tarandus*, a magnificent specimen of woodland caribou. Hunter Miller does a double take. She gives away no clue that the last time she saw anything like this was in the crosshairs of her rifle scope.

'One beautiful animal, isn't it? You'd be surprised how nimble and surefooted it can be travelling through the underbrush.'

'Lois Ann knows that well enough,' says Maude.

So it's not such a secret after all.

Lois Ann is quick to respond. 'I told you, the scope was off.' And a bit pissed that she's had to defend herself.

I can be very good at feigning confusion. As a teacher, I had years of practice.

Aiden comes to the rescue. 'Lois knows what she's at in the woods,' he points out. 'She told us she hunts big game.'

'Good for you.' What else can I say? 'What type of rifle do you use?'

'Let's not get into it.'

She's turned petulant, and the first thing in the morning. Not a good sign for the rest of the day.

We ease away from the entourage of mammals, towards something with less potential for combativeness.

'Well, butter my butt and call me a biscuit,' declares Lula. 'Will you look at that?'

The carcass of a giant squid in preserving fluid, extended its full 10 metres in a long, narrow tank. Safe to assume that Lois Ann has never had her scope trained on one of these.

The woman of the hour goes off on her own, to escape the others and explore the terrain. There's plenty more of Newfoundland's natural history to see, including more sea life of course, and the abundant seabird population.

The winged species are particular favourites of the McVickers. I'm not surprised. They have the birder look about them. I overhear their excitement and I have to smile.

'Look, Aiden. A *tickleace*.'

Maude not only recognized the bird, she also called it by its local name. *The Dictionary* continues to serve her well.

'Kittiwake, dear.'

'*Tickle-ass*,' she counters.

Another local name for the bird, the crude one.

Aiden surreptitiously runs his fingers over his wife's butt. She giggles. I wish I hadn't seen that.

I stand there and think here are old-age pensioners from Ontario likely getting it on like nobody's business. Probably jumping into bed at the drop of a hat, hauling out the sex toys and going at it til the cows come home. While virile, not-yet-fifty yours truly is left whistling Dixie.

Sad. Even if there is a morsel of comfort to be found in the thought of past liaisons. Even if I know that sex is an answer to only some of life's woes. Even if I know that self-pity in itself is sad. Let me go around in circles and see how fast I get there.

'*Sébastien?*'

There's music in a name. 'Yes, Renée.'

Ever-individualistic Renée has drawn herself away from the natural history component of the museum, and taken up with the storyboards and artifacts of Newfoundland's early European contact. She is surprised there was such a strong French presence. She is standing in front of a model of their principal fortification.

'Look. *Plaisance*. Such a lovely name to call their barricade.'

We both know the name translates to something pleasurable. If pleasurable Renée is out to make a point, it has been made.

Suddenly, my phone vibrates in my pocket. It's like a current through my genitals.

I excuse myself and go outside to answer it.

It's Olsen. 'I just sent you a picture. Did you get it?'

I check. 'Yes.' I look more closely at the image of two people standing someplace with mountains in the background. 'That's Graham. A few years younger but definitely him. And the woman. My God, it's Lois Ann.'

'That's what I thought. It's not Lois. It's Mira, his wife.'

'They could be sisters.'

'Not only could be. I'd say they'd have to be. If not twins.'

The picture was taken several years ago outside the Banff Springs Hotel, in the Rocky Mountains. Olsen doesn't tell me how he discovered this or how he even got his hands on the picture. Cops, as we all know, have their ways.

'Then why wasn't there any sign of recognition between Lester and Lois on the trail? They acted like they'd never met before.'

'My guess is they were having an affair, but Lester was just being very careful not to make it public, so there was no chance of it ever getting back to Mira. And who knows, maybe it wasn't hard for him to keep his distance. Maybe all he cared about was the sex.'

Right. 'Okay, so let's buy into the affair business. In that case, why wasn't Lois devastated when Lester got killed?'

'Because she didn't give a shit about him. She lured him on the tour so he could be bumped off. Could be she and Mira are in cahoots.'

'Working together to get the job done on Lester? You're kidding?'

The silence at the other end borders on smugness.

'So Mira wasn't in love with the bastard.' I'm backtracking. Flexing some verbal muscle, sounding more hard-boiled. Hitting Olsen at his own gut level. 'Maybe they both hated the son-of-a-bitch. Who the fuck knows?'

'Not us. Not yet. We've also been in touch with the RCMP in Red Deer. The Mounties have been questioning Lois's neighbours.'

Busy as bloody beavers. 'And?'

'Nothing. So far. I'll keep you posted. How's it going at your end?'

'Seems to me she's isolating herself from the rest of the group.'

'Interesting. Think she smells you poking around?'

I don't say anything. I can be as silently self-righteous as he can.

I'm not about to have Olsen think anything but that I'm tactfully zeroing in for the kill—the big blunder on the part of the unsuspecting Lois Ann. My strategy is to cool it for the rest of the time in The Rooms and over lunch, then resume maneuvers in the afternoon. Synard is not without a plan.

We are all feeling the urge to be out and about. The afternoon brings us to several kilometres of walking trail through the heart of the city. Lois Ann is especially anxious to get limbs in motion. She doesn't do well without exercise.

We begin the trail at the mouth of Quidi Vidi Lake, not far from The Plantation where we were yesterday. It's a couple of kilometres along one side of the lake, to where the trail continues west, and along Rennie's River.

We have not long set off when Lois Ann starts to get agitated. The rest of us are not walking fast enough for her. Her neuromuscular synapses are overwound. A cat on hot bricks.

She has an idea. She could do a circle of the lake and by the time she catches up with us we'll have made it down one side, to where we leave the lake for another part of the trail. The suggestion is hardly out of her mouth when she's off, arms pumping. From time to time we catch a glimpse of her in the distance, sucking back the oxygen, while the rest of us move along at our own clip, the McVickers and their walking poles setting the pace, Lula keeping up nicely, Renée being Renée. I'm better off walking beside her, rather than viewing her body in motion.

'*Sébastien*, Quidi Vidi—such a strange name.'

'It's from the Portuguese fishermen when they first landed here—*porto qui dividi*, the port that divides.'

'The port that divides? Divides what?'

I have never thought about *what*. I shrug. 'You know the Portuguese.'

She smiles. Not that the answer satisfies her.

'It divided us. You know, Lois Ann, off on her own.' I'm deliberately grasping at straws. Let's see where this leads. 'What's with Lois Ann?'

'What do you mean, *Sébastien*?'

'I mean, she can be, you know, a little aggressive.'

It seems to catch Renée unawares. 'Really?'

'You haven't noticed?' I'm being unprofessional—speaking to one client about another in this way—but I have to tease out all I can about Lois Ann.

'Not nice, *Sébastien*. She is herself, that is all. We are all our own person.' When I turn to read her expression, she looks at me with mild annoyance.

It's as if I've offended a friend. I wouldn't have thought the group had bonded so well. Then she smiles at me. Renée can be more than a little devilish.

When we reach the head of the lake, Lois Ann hasn't yet caught up with us. We wait at the spot where we'll cross the street to continue the trail along Rennie's River. I fill the time with an impromptu chat about what happens at Quidi Vidi Lake on the first Wednesday of August each year. 'The site of the Royal St. John's Regatta, the oldest continuous sporting event in North America, with records of the first boat races going back to at least 1816.'

Their attention suddenly shifts away from me. A police car, its siren blaring, races past us, followed a few seconds later by an ambulance. Both heading down the street that runs parallel to the length of the lake.

When, after several minutes, Lois Ann still hasn't shown up, we are all hit with the same thought.

'You folks stay here. I'll turn back and see what's up.'

I head off, picking up the pace, from a fast walk to an out-of-shape jog. It's not long before I catch sight of the flash bar of the police car, where it has stopped just past the mouth of the lake. I pump my pace up another notch, and five minutes later I arrive on the scene, very much out of breath, but managing to catch a glimpse of the person on the stretcher, being transported from the trail, past the trees, to the street where the ambulance is waiting.

It is Lois Ann. Head fallen to one side, eyes closed. Hastily, I explain to the cop who I am.

'Her vitals are all good. Still in shock. She says a man jogged up behind her, deliberately ran into her, forcing her off the trail, where she fell to the ground. He stole her wallet from the pouch around her waist and ran off.

'Did she get a look at him?'

'Apparently not. She fell face first into the undergrowth. Someone discovered her and called 9-1-1.'

By this time the stretcher is in the ambulance. 'Which hospital?'

'Health Sciences. You want to come with me?'

I explain about the others. He takes my contact information.

'She should be okay. Shock more than anything. Likely they'll want to keep her overnight for observation.'

'I'll make it to the hospital as soon as I can.'

He's gone, trailing the ambulance, and I'm on my way back to the remainder of the group. By the time I get to them they know something is up. They're stunned, again.

I'm down to four clients, but still holding on.

We curtail the walk in favour of a drink. We all take the time to decompress. I manage to find a private moment to call Olsen and tell him what's happened. He's thinking what I'm thinking—that Lois Ann may be around for longer than she counted on.

When the five of us climb the narrow wooden stairs to The Crow's Nest bar it's empty except for a couple of people at a corner table, and the bartender. She's a sweetheart, never anything but pleasant and invariably good for a chat. I've been coming here a lot since the divorce, when I need a drink and am in no mood for a loud bar and its louder music.

We order drinks and take to the leather chairs that form a

square in front of the fireplace. 'The Crow's Nest is a National Historic Site and here we are surrounded by artifacts, from all these wooden ship's badges covering the walls to the periscope from German U-boat 190, which surrendered just south of the city at the end of the war.'

Aiden is especially fascinated. His father was in the war, he tells us. 'Survived, thankfully, though he was partially disabled. He lost the use of his right hand when the Canadians fought their way through Italy. Before the war he had his mind set on becoming a lawyer. He still could have I suppose, but never did.'

The surroundings seem to have triggered something in him. It is strange how people, put in an odd circumstance, will open up their personal lives.

'He always felt held back from making a decent living. We never had much money growing up, and he felt he had failed us.'

'Life is never fair,' adds his wife. 'Plans can fly out the window just as quick as that.' Maude snaps her fingers, which strikes me as curious for a woman of her age. As if in another life she had been a jazz singer, which she was decidedly not. She realizes the others are staring at her, including her husband. 'Take Lois Ann,' she says. 'I wonder if she'll ever climb another mountain. I hope there's nothing broken.'

'I don't think so. When I talked to the policeman, he sounded optimistic. It was shock more than anything.'

'If it had been me,' says Lula, 'I'd have whipped the bugger in the dangly bits with my cane.'

None of us doubt her for a minute. There's an inaudible moan as I cross my legs. Renée smiles.

Lula is able to find humour in any situation. You got to love her for that. No doubt she has stories of her own to tell. I'm curious. For starters, how did she ever end up on this tour?

'A broken heart,' she says.

'A broken heart?'

'Yes, siree, Bob.'

She loves it when she has an audience.

'In fact his name was Bob. Robert Adams Junior. And, as it turned out, the Senior was an asshole, too.'

'*Très intéressant.*' Renée is as ripe for the story as any of us.

'Boyfriend Bob was in the United States Air Force. Master Sergeant Robert Adams. He always insisted on the *Robert*. That should have been my first clue. It wasn't. I was in love. Hopelessly in love, and nothing to do in the '50s but wait for him to return to the States after his posting overseas. Newfoundland looked so exotic, postmarked on the envelopes.'

We can all sense what's coming. Lula recounts the nasty deed, stiffened upright in the chair, supporting herself with her cane, as if it had all happened yesterday.

'He came back, of course. With a sweet young foreign gal on his arm. Oh, she was a catch all right. Her pappy had more money than Robert Adams, the First, although, as it turned out, even that was not near as much as the old fart pretended it was. I had been warned, in a letter that arrived two days before they did. There was nothing for me to do—I had no claim; we weren't engaged—nothing to do but quit my job at the head office at the Adams' Cotton Mills, slam the door, and hightail it back home to Jonesborough.'

She pauses there. It's not an unfamiliar story. The Americans set up several military bases in Newfoundland and Labrador during WWII, before we became part of Canada. They stayed open for years afterwards. I had an aunt who married a GI and moved to Colorado, one of 40,000 local girls who married American servicemen over the years. 'If you can't get a man, get a Yank,' was the old adage. Likely started by jilted local fellows, horny and at the wrong end of the love line.

'You never married?' asks Maude.

'Nope. What you see is what you get.'

I'm not sure any man would have wanted to tackle her. Of course, who's to say what she was like in her prime. Beneath her eighty-one years could have been a very good-looking young woman. It is not hard to image that.

Renée has discreetly shed a few tears. 'It's sad, Lula. Men can be so cruel. I've had two, I should know.'

Two. I'm not surprised. Oh well, here we go. As if Aiden and I are not in the room. Aiden has had his share of tarnished domestic bliss I can tell. And, as for me, I'm not about to go there in front of people I've known for two days and likely will never see again.

'We're a cheery lot,' I tell them. 'Another drink anyone?'

'Why not,' says Lula. 'Another Jack D for me. Straight up.' There are seconds all around.

By the time we leave the Crow's Nest we're feeling all the mellower for our visit. The cab drops us at the Delta. They're all due a catnap before we meet up later for the evening meal.

I head to the hospital to check on Lois Ann. She's resting comfortably enough. In fact she's asleep, in a room with another patient who is more than eager to chat.

'She's hardly stirred since they brought her in. When she did wake up, she said hello, and turned her face to the wall. I heard the nurse say she's not from here. Mainlander, is she? Not hard to tell.'

'Alberta.'

'Lots of Newfoundlanders in Alberta. But she can't be one of us.'

'When she does wake up, would you tell her Sebastian came by.'

'You better write that down. I'm not good on foreign names. You're not from Newfoundland then, are you?'

'Just describe what I look like. That'll be enough.'

'Oh my, a bit huffy, are we? I'll tell her mid-fifties and going bald.'

I snigger and quickly exit the room before I decide to snap at her and she presses her help button. At the nurse's station I find out Lois Ann is doing fine. No injuries except for a minor bruise. Still a little in shock, and they are keeping her overnight. The doctor will see her in the morning, and if all goes according to plan she should be released by the afternoon.

Just in time to pack up and head for the airport.

In the parking lot, I call Olsen.

'I already know. Her name activated the system and the report popped up in my inbox.'

Police efficiency never ceases to amaze me.

'She didn't say much,' he tells me. 'Probably nothing more than you already know.' There it is again. He has a record of what the cop on the scene has told me. I wonder if Olsen knows what aftershave I'm wearing.

'There goes my access to the suspect. I could go visit her in the hospital in the morning.'

'No point. She's clammed up. Shock gives her the perfect reason to do so.'

'Do you think she faked being mugged?'

'Hard to tell. I wouldn't be surprised either way.'

'That's not very cop-like.'

I can feel the glare at the other end.

'What do *you* think?'

'I think you could be barking up the wrong tree. What about the jogger? Jogger at the scene of the fall. Jogger at the scene of the mugging. Maybe the same person.'

'No luck locating either one of them.'

'Which tells you they made a deliberate effort to get away.'

'Not necessarily in the case of jogger number one. And we

don't know if there ever was a jogger number two. And if there was one, and the two joggers are the same guy, what would be his motive in coming back to harass another one of the tour group? Follow me?'

Gotta love that urge to itemize. 'A reasonable point,' I admit.

'Ms. Miller remains the prime suspect.'

'But you have no solid evidence to charge her.'

'Not at this point.'

'You have hope?'

'We follow the leads, and go until we can go no farther.'

Sounds like an inspirational poster on his office wall. 'Which means?'

'Which means there are questions yet to be answered.'

'And I'm off-duty.'

'I'm afraid it's out of your hands. You've been a great help.'

I feel a handshake looming.

'I'll drop the invoice in the mail.'

He chuckles. 'Let's get together for a beer sometime.'

How sweet. A sudden urge to revamp his image to something more charming.

'I'll keep in touch,' he adds.

'I'm holding my breath. Starting now.'

'Sebastian,' he hesitates, but says it anyway, 'you need to loosen up.'

What I need to do is hang up. 'Good-bye.'

I'm at home, thinking I need a Scotch. Gaffer thinks I don't. He's ready to play the game of throwing his squeaky ball, him racing to snatch it, and me chasing him around the house trying to grab it out of his mouth so I can throw it again. I tire of this long before he ever does.

He doesn't appreciate seeing me collapse on the couch, and he leaps from the floor onto my chest and starts licking my face. I have an aversion to dog tongues. But I can't say I don't appreciate the affection.

Now the mutt's in need of me taking him for a walk. I've discovered that some days walking Gaffer is a deeply satisfying experience, Zen-like, almost. Yoga on a leash.

I live very close to Government House, which, in colonial days, was home to the governors sent from England. It's now where the province's Lieutenant-Governor hangs out. The grounds are open to the public during the day. Gaffer does his business, but it's with utmost respect.

When we return home, my stress level reduced, Nicholas is sitting on the living-room couch, device-less and looking miserable.

'Welcome, back. You seem to have a magnetic attraction to this house.'

I smile. Gaffer runs and jumps into his lap. He licks the boy's face furiously. It doesn't help the situation.

I sit on the couch next to Nicholas and put my hand on his knee. He leans into me.

'You know this won't go over well with your mother.'

'I don't care.'

'But you have to care. There's an agreement in place.'

'How come I don't have a say?'

'You did, at the time. Don't you remember. You told the judge it was okay.'

'Things change.'

'But you have to play by the rules.'

'I hate it when she brings him home.'

'Who?'

'The cop.'

'Is that what you call him?'

'No. He wants me to call him Fred. I don't call him anything.'

I steel myself. 'He could be a nice guy.' I manage not to
choke on the words, which is good.

'I thought you hated him.'

'Who said that?'

'Mom.'

'I don't hate him.'

'But you don't like him?' Is that hope in his voice?

'We get along.'

Nicholas seems to know that Olsen has been involved in
the situation with Lester. I wasn't the one who told him.

All this is going nowhere. The fact remains that his mother
will be phoning any minute, then she'll show up at the house
and set off another round of fireworks. None of which I need
right now.

'You get ten minutes. Then I'm going to drop you back
home.'

'I won't go.'

'Nicholas. Pal. This is not good. You'll see Gaffer tomorrow at lunchtime. And then come by after school. The tour will
be over. I'll be home.'

In the end he gets in the car without a fight. When we
arrive at the house, he doesn't let me hug him, and when he
gets out of the car, he doesn't look back. It's okay. A bit hard to
take, but, for the moment, okay.

The meal is at 7:30 at Chinched Bistro. It's within walking
distance of the hotel and we could all do with the fresh air. The
restaurant is on Bates Hill, not far from the infamous George
Street with its wall-to-wall pubs. George Street is dead at this
hour, but it won't be when it's time for us to return to the hotel.

Lula's eyes brighten at the thought, although I'm not sure it's for real.

I've eaten here several times before. For appetizers I convince them to go with the pig ear fries and the awesome house-made charcuterie board. They are in no mood to resist.

They are a somber lot. I tell them what I know about Lois Ann's condition, which is very little, but they appear satisfied that she'll make her flight home tomorrow.

'This is peanuts for someone who's climbed Kilimanjaro,' says Lula blandly.

'We've enjoyed Newfoundland, if not the circumstances,' says Aiden, after vacantly consuming the bulk of the pig's ear fries.

I sense a restlessness for tomorrow and an end to the tour.

'What's ahead for everyone?'

They're noncommittal. As if it were nothing much I'd be interested in.

'Same old, same old,' says Lula.

Renée gives her French shoulders a shrug. '*La routine.*'

And as for those from London, Ontario, 'Life goes on.'

It does, but apparently with not much enthusiasm. By the time we finish with the appetizers and take on the mains, conversations have settled in on the weather and the price of gasoline.

I'm determined to pull them out of the doldrums. 'What say we skip dessert and head to George Street?'

They're no more enthusiastic. Except for intrepid Lula. I'm not deterred.

The two pedestrian blocks of George Street have more drinking establishments per square metre than any other street in North America. Few people *get on the go*, to use the local vernacular, much before midnight, but then again George Street in high gear can be a bit raunchy for the McVickers of the world.

I connect to George Street where it meets Water, the others following dutifully behind. We skirt Yellowbelly Brewery and Public House and head deeper into the street, past Trapper John's, past Bridie Molloy's, the Rock House, as far as O'Reilly's.

The change of scenery seems to have pumped new life into the funereal four, especially outside O'Reilly's, with its Irish-Newfoundland Music roaring onto the street. Maude offers petty resistance, but in the end flings her arms around her husband and coerces him into dancing. Not that he shows much resistance. The McVickers are soon two-stepping with an expertise that makes me think they were the top students in their seniors dance class back in London. They go practically unnoticed, it being George Street, where the bar life constantly spills into the outdoors. And nothing to what the twenty-somethings will be getting up to come midnight.

My destination is another bar along the street, said to host the best Screech-In Ceremony in Newfoundland. Screech is a brand of Caribbean rum, long blended and bottled here. The Screech-In is meant to be a comic ceremony that will turn any tourist into an *honourary Newfoundlander*. I'm no fan of the Screech-In. It perpetuates the stereotype of the rip-roaring, simple-minded Newfoundlander.

Now it's big business. You sign up and pay your twenty bucks and you get to be Screeched In. So who's got the simple mind now? Not the owner.

There's a method to my hypocrisy. If there is anything that might bring the crew back to life it's the Screech-In.

The ceremony is due to start in half an hour. They're skeptical, although since I'm the one forking over the blood money, and they are but four of the dozen signing up, they agree to it. That's the first step. The next is to buy them all a drink. Another freebie they can't resist. Step three is to plant them among the crowd and hope it boosts their energy level a few notches.

I give Lula credit for being the one to break the mould. The bourbon helps. She's into her third by the time the Screech-In begins.

The MC is a stand-up comic in a sou'wester. His first order of business is to get the dozen potential honourees, many with accents of their own, to speak in Newfoundland dialect. The test phrase is: 'Deed I is, me ol' cock. Long may yer big jib draw.' Maude's translation: Indeed I am, my old friend. Long may there be wind in your sails. Bit stiff, but the woman must still be up nights reading her dictionary.

To me it's centuries-old gibberish dug up to feed the tourists. I'm already cringing, but I'll admit that the MC has skillfully built a riot of fun, getting all of them to repeat the phrase as best they can. The alcohol cuts inhibitions by half. And I won't deny that hearing it delivered by a boozed-up bloke from Perth is a laugh.

'And what's your name, my love?'

'Lula.'

'Where you from, Lula, my love?'

'Tennessee.'

'And what brings you to Newfoundland?'

'It ain't the weather.'

The fellow senses he's caught a good one at the end of his line. 'A man? You come here to find a man to take back home.'

'You got it. Know any lusty young feller who might be interested in a gal in her eighties?'

The crowd is loving it, and Lula is willing to play it for all it's worth.

'What about me?' says the MC.

'You got money?'

'I was just about to ask you the same question.'

'Some jerk stole it on me.'

'I won't go there, Lula, my love.' Laughter all around. 'Anyone in the room with money willing to team up with a mature older lady from Tennessee?'

'I bake a mean buttermilk pie.'

More laughter. 'No takers, I'm afraid. Let's give a big hand for Lula from Tennessee!'

The applause is rife with mock catcalls, which must do an eighty-one-year-old good at some level. Off goes the MC to the next person.

All through the rest of the Screech-In—munching on a chunk of fried bologna, kissing a codfish hauled out for the occasion from a freezer, and finally downing a shot of Screech—I'm trying to get my head around Lula's comment about a man stealing her money. Perhaps it was nothing more than a joke.

Or perhaps it was a slip of her tongue and alcoholic mind. Before I get them back to the Delta, I step outside the bar and make a quick call to Olsen.

'You said any time.'

'What's up?'

I tell him. 'What do you make of it?'

'No Lula Jones or Tallulah Jones on the list of Lester's clients.'

'Changed her name to come on the trip?'

'No one from Tennessee as I recall.'

How dense is this man? It's getting late. I allow him that much.

'She lies. She fakes an accent. She fakes the whole Southern shtick. It's all an act.'

'She and Lois are a team. Whoever gets the opportunity first sends him flying over the cliff?'

'Could be.'

'You're thinking like a cop. That could be dangerous.'

'We're about to walk back to the hotel. She's half soused. Maybe there's more to come.'

'I'll go back to the list of clients. See if there's a way to find out their ages. I won't be able to do that until tomorrow.'

'You relax. You're off duty. Find something to take your mind off being a cop.'

I imagine what and hang up.

Inside, the gang of four have set their empty glasses on the bar in expectation of their leader's reappearance. All's well, except that Renée is having to keep Lula upright on one side, while her cane does the job on the other. She's had a few too many. She needs to sleep it off.

Once outside, Lula takes to singing. The Southern twang has disappeared. Grand Ole Opry it's not. I shouldn't read much into that. Singers take on the original cadence of a song, although an octogenarian singing The Beatles has its own freakishness.

It's the *Money* that gets me. That's what she wants. Forget the birds and the bees. Yeah.

The other three attempt to put a lid on it, to no good end.

'Lula, darling,' Renée appeals. No response. 'You're hurting my ears.'

It's a further call to arms for her vocal cords. The soulful word *money* belted several different ways.

Maude takes a turn. 'Lula, this is mortifying.'

There's no stopping her from belting it out, down and dirty. Money seems to have a wicked hold on her psyche.

Finally, Aiden reaches his breaking point. 'For God's sake, shut up!'

His admonishment clangs down the street. Then dead silence from all of us. Except for a moan from Lula that is threatening to turn into a whimper.

'I'm sorry, Lula.'

'Sorry is not good enough, Aiden.'

I'm not hearing the accent. Unfortunately, we are almost at the end of the street. It intersects Queen Street and we turn up to reach New Gower, where the unsuspecting Delta awaits.

Full-blown dissent within the ranks. An ugly little scenario. I'd like to think that all that's needed is a cooling-off period.

We enter the front door of the Delta looking noticeably thunderstruck. The concierge smiles, determinedly. 'Good evening, everyone.'

I'm the only one to return the smile. The others muddle off to the bank of elevators, splitting into two pairs before they get there, and not bothering to say goodnight, except for Renée.

A conscientious tour guide should know if Lula is no worse for her booze-up. 'I'll stick around the hotel for a while... in case I'm needed.' They don't make octogenarians like they used to.

'Sir,' says the concierge, drawing me back to something nearing normal.

'Yes?'

'Your group is checking out tomorrow I believe.'

'That's the plan.'

'A package arrived this afternoon for Mr. Lester. The one he was waiting for, I assume. Shall I contact the police? It's addressed to him, in care of something called *On the Rocks*.'

'Is the S at the end in brackets?'

'As a matter of fact it is.'

'That would be me. It's my touring business. I'll take it.'

'Are you sure? Shouldn't the pol...'

'Absolutely.'

He retrieves it from behind his desk. It's a small FedEx envelope.

'His son arrives tomorrow to accompany the body back to Toronto. I'll deliver it to him.'

The concierge is still uncertain. The envelope is no closer to being in my hands.

'It's in the contract.'

'The contract?'

'His tour contract. Section 5b. Any personal items left behind by mistake after the tour ends will be returned to the client at the client's expense.'

'But he's dead.'

'In this case, the next of kin.' The envelope makes a tentative move towards me. 'I'll waiver the bit about him having to pay.'

There. Have it. Finally.

'And would you be good enough to point me in the direction of the bar, my friend.'

My go-to Scotch is Lagavulin. They have the standard sixteen-year-old. And at this price, a single will have to do.

I settle into a corner, withdraw my phone from my pocket and place it on the table, beside the envelope, the back of which stares at me. The envelope's been sent by priority courier but still didn't arrive when he expected. I can see why. The return address is a Best Western hotel on some *rue* that I can't pronounce. In Paris.

The phone rings. It's Renée. 'I'm in the hotel lobby. We need to talk. Where are you?'

'The bar.'

'I'll find it.'

She arrives, looking a bit rumpled. Not like Renée. I suspect it was a tussle to get Lula in her room and settled away for the night.

'What would you like? White wine?'

She's looking at the FedEx envelope, but referring to the glass next to it. 'Is that Scotch?'

'Lagavulin. I don't think you would like it. It's smoky.'

'I'll have a double.'

Lula must have really been a handful. What can I say? I go to the bar and order it. For Renée I'll let the profit margin plunge even further.

The double does prove ambitious. The first swallow sets her back a few notches.

'Would you like water with it?'

'Never.'

Never? Really? 'Not even a little?'

'I need time out.'

Really?

'I need to. . .how you say. . .hang loose.'

Really?

Renée and I depart the bar together and find ourselves on the couch in my living room. I'll get to the envelope later. Much later, I hope.

Gaffer, the little bugger, is not cooperating, but piling his dish high with the pork/sweet potato/carrot concoction keeps him occupied while I slip back to the couch and offer Renée another drink.

'Do you have Macallan?'

She's been keeping this penchant for Scotch at bay. Its sudden revelation makes her all the more fascinating. I could play Nick Charles to her Nora quite willingly.

'Will Glenfarclas do?'

'In a pinch.' She smiles. That warm, succulent smile.

We're getting more comfortable on the couch, Gaffer

curled up to the right of me notwithstanding. Renée's tight to me on the left, glass in one hand, my thigh being stroked by the other hand.

This is shaping up very well indeed.

'What are your dreams, *Sébastien*, your ambitions?'

She means beyond the next hour. It's hard to go there when all the hormones are clamouring for short-term attention. If that hand of hers edges any higher, that part of my brain will likely pass into oblivion.

'Let's just say I'm working them out.'

'But where is it leading? You are divorced, but is there another woman in your life?'

'Not at the moment.'

'There should be. And together you could make the world your oyster.'

Where the hell are you going with this, Renée? I think it. I don't get around to saying it.

'I'm fond of oysters,' is what comes out. 'And I'm fond of you.' Lame and lamer.

Her hand wanders. Those probing, beautifully manicured red nails could do a lot of damage.

'Come with me.' I lead her up the partially lit stairs, together with the bottle of Scotch, her wayfaring hand in mine, her bare feet alighting the carpet provocatively, both sets of nails matched in what I can only think of as Parisian red. They are like touches of fire. And I'm just the lad who could use the heat.

Trotting up behind us is the furry beast. Sorry, Gaffer, you're on your own, pal, and I shut the bedroom door firmly behind us before he has a chance to sneak inside.

I set the bottle of Scotch on the bedside table. There is a supply of clean Glencairn glasses scattered about the house, in anticipation of just such an occasion. It includes a pair in the medicine cabinet of the en suite.

The bed is a bit rumpled. Had I known, I would have changed the sheets, though for now it is all about giving in to this moment atop the duvet, a sliver of light escaping past the edge of the bathroom door. My Joe Boxers stiffen with considerable confidence, threatening to double the font size imprinted on the waist band.

'I like a man with *vigueur*.'

'*C'est moi*, Renée. *C'est moi*.'

We lie about the bed, spent amid the afterglow, Renée's breasts pressed tight to my back, her manicured fingers interlaced with my fingers and resting against my chest. We've migrated to one side of the bed, freeing half the duvet to throw over us. In my drift in and out of sleep I feel this could be Paris. Something vague in my state of sleep euphoria, something about my very own *Arc de Triomphe*.

'I need a drink, *Sébastien*.'

'Really, darling?' The words are dense with drowsiness.

'Please, will you get some glasses?'

'In the medicine cabinet.'

'Thanks, darling. I will be waiting right here for you.'

Not what I am wanting to hear. Getting out of bed is a rough task, getting to the bathroom even rougher. When I return, naked except for the pair of Glencairn glasses held to my chest, nipple height, and very vaguely erotic, Renée is sitting up in bed, the Glenfarclas bottle in her hand.

With her other hand she holds up the duvet, inviting me back under. I am now awake.

'We must celebrate,' she says. She pours a generous dram in each glass, then leans over me to set the bottle on the bedside table. I don't miss the opportunity to kiss each darling breast.

'To *Sébastien*.'

'To Renée.'

Glasses raised. Glasses clinked.

A scratch at the door. A knock at the door.

What the sweet fuck?

'Dad. It's me.'

Good God Almighty.

'Nicholas!'

'Can I come in?'

'No!'

'I need to see you.'

'Go downstairs.' I'm already struggling into my pants. 'I'm on my way.' And I'm not very fuckin pleased.

I grab a shirt and swing open the door, shutting it and Renée behind me.

'Nicholas, what the hell are you doing here? It's after midnight!'

He's sitting on the couch crying, Gaffer tight in his arms. A pair of open-toed heels slouch on the carpet across from him. I attempt to push them out of sight with my foot, hoping the tears have marred his vision.

'Never mind,' he says, catching a sob. 'I know someone is here.'

'Nicholas, man, what the hell is going on?'

'I…I…I won't stay.'

I sit next to him. He fights against my attempt to put an arm around him. I hold him tight until he gives in.

'I need an explanation.'

'The asshole has moved in.'

I don't need to ask.

'I don't want him there.'

'It's not your call. Your mother and I are divorced. Your mother has a right—'

'I don't care. He's an idiot. They don't think I hear them but I do.'

Where the hell do I go with that?

'I come here and now you're…'

'That's enough.'

He doesn't take it any further. Thankfully.

'Adults are entitled…'

'To screw around.'

'Nicholas, pal…'

'I'm not dumb, you know. You need your sex.'

Good God. My hand is on top of my head, pressing down, as if I could make my mind contract.

'See what I mean.'

'What *I* mean is that life is very complicated. And you need to find your own way through it.'

'I'm trying.'

The two words break my heart.

Of course he's trying. Of course I need to help him through that.

But he can't sneak out of his house at midnight and show up at my place any time he wants.

'I tried texting. You didn't answer.'

He's right. I had the phone turned off. So I wouldn't be disturbed…*we* wouldn't be disturbed.

'You're going to have to go back home.'

'I know.' He wipes his eyes and looks at me. 'Can I have ten more minutes with Gaffer?' I'm not answering. 'Can I? You can go back upstairs if you want.'

I glare at him, unsmiling.

I drop him at Samantha's and wait outside until I'm sure he's in the house. When I get back Renée is dressed, her slim legs ending in her open-toed heels. She's sitting on the couch, legs crossed.

'In France kids would know better.'

Not appreciated. But I don't say anything.

'Sit down. Have a drink with me before I get you to call me a taxi.'

She has her near-empty glass in her hand. Mine is sitting on the end table. I ignore it. I'm not in the drinking mood.

She insists. '*Tchin, tchin*,' she says, holding up her glass, waiting to have it clink with mine.

I pick up the glass, if only to end the night on a neutral note.

'*Santé, Sébastien.* You were very good.'

What is this—she has a rating system? She feels the need to boost my ego?

I'm preoccupied, distracted. My head is not my own. I wander into the kitchen to get away from her for the moment. I dump the contents of the glass into the sink and when I return I set the empty glass back on the end table.

'You were very good as well, Renée.'

I'm on the phone, calling her a cab, while Gaffer, who has been lying quietly in his orthopedic bed up to now, wanders over and begins licking her exposed red toes.

'Get away. Get away!' And then she takes a swipe at him, coloured toes grazing his ribs. Gaffer yelps.

I snatch him from the floor and into my arms.

'Disgusting creature,' she mutters.

I bite my tongue, only because there is still time remaining in the tour. Renée exits the house, and into the back seat of the taxi, without saying anything more.

Neither do I, dammit.

Not so Gaffer. He sits in my arms barking loudly until the taxi is down the street and out of sight.

'Good dog. Good dog.'

Before I go to bed, I text Nicholas. 'You okay?'

Not long after, 'I'm cool.'

'Nite. Love ya.'

'Love ya too.'

Now I'll sleep okay. The smell of Renée's perfume is a distraction, but I allow Gaffer onto the bed. He could do with a bath. It helps mask the odour.

It's morning and I'm in the shower before I remember Lester's envelope. Towel around me, still half-wet, I'm parading around the house, trying to remember where I put it. It's nowhere to be found.

I'm certain I didn't leave it at the bar. I get dressed and go outside and search the car. Nothing.

And again the house. Still nothing.

One explanation circles my mind. Renée. For whatever reason, she stole it. Her handbag was certainly big enough to conceal the envelope.

There's something up. Do I confront her when I get to the hotel later in the morning? If she did take it she'd simply deny it and I'd have no access to her room to prove otherwise. And I can't call asshole Olsen since he's the one who should have possession of the envelope. I feel myself floundering towards a brick wall.

Besides, I am supposed to meet them at 9:30 and it's after 8 and I need to go to the hospital and see what's up with Lois.

Normally I'd take Gaffer for a morning walk before I leave the house. No time, except a minute in what passes for a back-yard so he can do his business. 'Sorry, kid. Nick will be by in a few hours. Hold the fort.' I toss him an extra couple of treats, and I'm out the front door and on my way. Except once I get in the car I realize I forgot my sunglasses. Ryan, the weather guy, did promise sun all day. I'll need them.

The nursing staff at Health Sciences is not thrilled to see me arrive so early in the morning. Visiting hours don't start until 11, but there it is, what can I do but pretend I work for the RNC and stress that the visit will be short and to the point. As it turns out Lois/Lois Ann isn't in her room. She has been taken to the x-ray unit.

Her roommate looks at me from the other side of her breakfast tray. 'Decided to rejoin the common folk, did we?'

I ignore it. 'Please tell Lois I came by and that I hope she's feeling better. Ask her to phone me if she's being released.' I leave her my card. 'She can call my cell.'

'I haven't got my glasses on. What's your name again?'

'Sebastian.'

'That's right. How could I forget? She said it enough times.'

I halt my move towards the door. She can see I need an explanation. She lets me dangle in anticipation.

'In her sleep. That name of yours, over and over. Not very flattering, I have to say.'

'I work for the RNC. I'll have to ask you to elaborate.'

'A cop. Oh, my.'

'Just tell me what she said.'

'She called you a...I'm afraid I can't say it out loud. Two words. First word begins with F, ends with G. Second word, compound word, first part begins with A, second part begins with H. Follow me?'

Only too well.

'Sometimes the second word was replaced with *idiot* or *moron*, sometimes with another compound word. First part begins with D, second part also begins with H. Follow me?'

I'm struggling.

'Another word for the male member. Rhymes with *prick*.' Her hand shoots to cover her mouth. 'Oh, my.' She crosses herself.

'Thank you.'

I leave the room, having fouled her breakfast, but with absolute certainty that Lois (Ann) has been up to no good.

My phone says 9:29 as I slip past the front door of the Delta. The concierge offers a tentative smile. Mine is forced, but broad and assertive. He retreats behind his desk.

There is no one at the usual meeting spot. No couple-most-eager, no hungover octogenarian, no dog kicker.

I wait ten minutes. No one. Very strange. Perhaps I got the time wrong.

The concierge can see I have been stood up. He wanders over. 'Do you wish me to make enquiries, sir? Should I call Miss Sipp's room?' he says, his smugness seeping through the cracks in his smile.

'I think not.' I stare at him, my smile as hypocritical as his own, until he moves off.

Now I am in the position of using my own phone to call and looking the idiot when no one answers, of waiting longer and looking even more abandoned.

I take the elevator to the fourth floor where all their rooms are located. I feel odd. Like a snoop. Private investigator sounds better.

The McVickers door is closed. I can't hear anything. On the other hand, Lula's room, even though the door is also closed, definitely has people inside, more than two, by the sound of it.

And as for Renée's, it's ajar, with the chambermaid's cart outside. As I stroll past I can see her maneuvering about the bed. Renée's flight to Heathrow is not until late this evening. The others are a bit earlier, but all the rooms are booked for another day, so they will be available to them when the tour ends.

I become inspired. There's a stairwell not far from the room. Outside another room is a pile of dirty plates, topped by three wine glasses, left over from room service the night before. It is merely a matter of lifting them discreetly from the carpet, positioning myself at the top of the stairwell, one foot keeping the door partially open to be sure the sound gets through, then sending the whole shebang crashing down the concrete stairs.

I edge quickly past the mess, race up one flight, emerge from the stairs to the fifth floor, then stroll to the elevators and take one back down to the fourth.

The chambermaid and her co-worker from an adjacent room are in a tizzy. One is on her cell to security, the other on her cell arguing about who is responsible for cleaning up the mess.

I slip inside Renée's room and take a quick look around. A suitcase lies open on a stand near the bed. I poke through the few items inside. Nothing. A cabinet houses the TV and a few shelves, empty except for bits of hiking gear. There's a dresser against a wall to the right of the window, open-toed heels standing defiantly upright next to it. I start in the bottom drawer and work my way up. Nothing. Nothing, Nothing. Bingo. Where else, under her thick arrangement of lacy underwear. Black and red only. There is no time to be distracted.

The envelope has been opened. I poke my hand inside and retrieve the single item. It looks to be a passport, but there's no time for anything but to slip it in a pocket, return the envelope and pile the lacies back where they were.

Then retreat from the room. Nicely done.

I'm thinking I have promise as a PI.

I take a deep breath and stroll back down the hall, well past Lula's room, until my heart rate nears normal.

I retrace my steps and stand outside Lula's door. There's a do-not-disturb sign hanging off the door knob.

Gentle knock.

'12:30. I told housekeeping 12:30.'

That deserves another knock. Louder this time.

'Can't you read the—'

Only when the door is open all the way does Lula see who it is.

'Sebastian.'

The noise level inside goes dead. Before long Lula is backed up by three others, demonstrating various degrees of bewilderment.

'Didn't we have a meeting scheduled? For 9:30.'

'My memory is not good. Drank too much I guess.' Lula turns and looks at the others.

'Wasn't it 10?' says Aiden.

'I'm sure it was 10,' says Maude.

I'm sure it wasn't. But the client is always right.

'Of course it was 10,' says Renée. 'I'll need to get changed.' She pushes past me and heads to her room.

Obviously they weren't expecting me at 9:30. Why? I don't know. Were they expecting me at 10? I don't know, and does it matter? A half hour is no big deal.

While I'm waiting in the lobby for them to get ready, one eye steady on the elevator doors, I discreetly remove the FedEx item from its safe haven and take a look. It is a passport. A Canadian passport in the name of Mira Elizabeth Campbell, born April 21, 1944 in Stoke-on-Trent, England. And yep, the sour passport picture is of the known but unseen Mira, Lester's widow.

I'll admit the passport is useless in my hands. I should put it in the hands of my ex-wife's live-in, scourge of my young son, and prick by any fair description.

I text said prick. *The smiling concierge at the delta has a document for you sent to Lester from Paris city of love. Arrived yesterday lucky I was able to put it in your hands ly2.*

I get an envelope at the front desk, write Olsen's name on it and seal the passport inside. The concierge takes it, as if he's doing me a favour instead of doing the job the hotel is overpaying him to do.

Fortunately for him, the elevator doors open and the fab four all emerge at the same time. They are each dragging a suitcase.

'You're checking out now?' They're all well aware the rooms are booked for another day.

'We decided to save you a little money,' says Aiden.

'And we have a plan,' adds Maude. The other two are already in the line-up at the checkout desk.

They'll do what they want to do. They arrange with the all-smiling concierge to store their luggage for later pick-up.

'So?' I am holding a copy of the itinerary in my hand. 'As *your* copies also point out, and I quote: 9:30—leave hotel for Botanical Gardens and Fluvarium. View firsthand the varied plant life of Newfoundland. Get up close and personal with our freshwater fish. Enjoy lunch at a Duckworth Street café. Stroll downtown and take in a few art galleries as the tour winds down.'

I lead them outside, away from the prying eyes of the concierge.

'Let's get it together, people. We have a few hours of the tour left. Let's make the most of them. As we say in Newfoundland: *Pessimists stay home. Optimists close the porch door behind them.*'

We don't really. I just made that up.

'We have something different in mind.' It's Lula, being her unusual forceful self.

What might that be? As if I haven't had enough surprises from them already.

'We need to see a whale and a *proper* iceberg before we go,' says Renée.

'And we need more exercise,' adds Maude. 'It's a long flight. Very long for some of us.'

'And frankly, I'd rather see the plant life in the wild,' says Lula. 'And Mother Nature is all the art I need.'

How thought-provoking you are, Lula.

'So to make a long story short,' says Aiden, 'we're proposing we all go to Cape Spear and hike the East Coast trail to Maddox Cove. We have the time. First flight is not until 7. We'll pay the shot. The taxi out and back. And we'll pick up something on the way and have lunch on the trail. What do you say, Sebastian?'

I'd say how the hell did they get this in their heads?

'We've seen pictures of the trail online,' adds his wife.

Can I argue with clients? No. Is it a reasonable proposal? If they say it is.

'It's been a rough tour for us all. You've been a trooper, Sebastian.'

With that Lula raises her cane in a call to action. It's like a wave of the baton striking up the band.

The McVickers take hold, with a new degree of enthusiasm. Their telescopic walking sticks are well in hand, causing a spike in their energy levels.

Our dear Miss Sipp is the least generous. I'm wondering if she checked the stolen FedEx envelope among her lacies when she packed her suitcase. To think that ten hours before she was flat on her back and counting her lucky stars that I had dropped into her life. I hate to break the news, Renée, but the man of your fantasies has turned real and he's not what you had in mind. He's a man with a son and a dog, neither of which you were willing to accommodate. But let's not go there.

As it stands I have two-thirds of a broken tour group with

issues, who seem to want to go out on a high note.

I finally nod and smile in agreement.

All four of them have a hand in the air to hail the taxi van that's parked nearby.

So here's for one final, unforgettable experience of *On the Rock(s)*, a quest that will overwhelm anything negative that they might have experienced, most of all the untimely, tragic, and ghastly death of a fellow participant.

I need to take charge at this point. I am the tour leader after all.

Joining me on the quest are:

Aiden McVickers, 67, of lovely London, Ontario, skeptic, potential troublemaker, man on a mission.

Maude McVickers, 69, also of lovely London, Ontario, obsessed with all things Newfoundland, resistant to thinking for herself, suppressed in more ways than one.

Lula Jones, may or may not be from Jonesborough, Tennessee, probably something less than 81, obsessed with money and making up for lost time.

Renée Sipp, of somewhere in France (still likely), a robust 45-55, flexible, a thief and an enigma.

And out of the picture is *Lois (Ann) Miller*, prime suspect in what could (possibly) be foul play.

What, if anything, either of the remaining four have to do with Lois remains to be determined. I am the one in the best position to find out, having as I do, this one last kick at the can. All bets are off. For the next few hours the RNC and Olsen are out of the picture. Sebastian Synard is on his own. As we say in Newfoundland, let's rock.

5

IT WILL TAKE a fifteen-minute taxi ride to reach Cape Spear from Rocket Bakery where Aiden has dodged in and picked up lunch for us all. It's not a particularly scenic drive and the driver is not a colourful townie, so it's a slow fifteen minutes. The driver is tall and thin and from Latvia. He looks as if he overdosed on basketball as a kid and never quite recovered. Gone are the days when you could count on a St. John's taxi driver being squat and corpulent, speak in an Irish-laced accent incomprehensible to tourists and thus providing solid entertainment for the full duration of the ride.

The last drive-through village before we break into the panorama of Cape Spear goes by the name of Blackhead. It's another of those Newfoundland place names that offers comic relief to Lula and her sort.

'Of course there's an explanation. It gets its name from Black Head, a particularly prominent headland.' All lost on her, who wouldn't know a headland from a footpath.

I need to take a deep breath and realign myself. It doesn't pay for a tour guide to turn venomous.

Focus, Sebastian, focus. Preempt the negative by starting the conversation and taking the lead thereafter.

The coastline suddenly opens before us, leading to the rising headland that forms the most easterly point in North America. It's one of those scenic jolts that sends the heart rates of tourism-ad makers soaring.

The seas are rough today, pounding ashore, smashing onto the rocks, sending saltwater spume far into the air. Nobody could have ordered up any better. I'm finally getting into the rhythm of the moment.

There's a small parking lot along the road leading to Cape Spear itself, and it's here we exit the van for the full-on experience. You don't come to Newfoundland and not feel the thrust of the moody brine against its shores. It was the sea that brought people here, it was the sea that sustained them for centuries, and it is the sea that can be our undoing. As we all well know.

'The North Atlantic is both friend and foe. Off these shores were once the best cod-fishing grounds in the world. The sea literally overflowed with fish and the Newfoundland fishery fed the world. Until greed devastated the stocks and the livelihoods of thousands were wiped away. Replaced by thousands more, an island born again, with oil as its economic saviour.'

Put me in front of a camera, I could be running for political office. Of course, no more than the next person on the street. Newfoundlanders breathe politics.

'Everyone has an opinion on why our history unfolded as it did, and every opinion has a smattering of truth. Look out at that ocean, and you'll see the truth behind them all. That sea can turn in your favour, and the next second betray you. Don't turn your back on the sea. You might forever pay the price.'

'Amen,' says Lula, with a little less fervour than before.

Aiden nods his head, but it is Maude who is most affected. There are tears in her eyes as they look far out upon the ocean.

Only Renée seems to lack any reaction. Within a few seconds I discover I've underestimated her.

'*Sébastien*, there is poetry in your soul.'

And what might that mean? Coming from a thief in the night, I'm not sure. I suspect she is up to no good, again.

Back in the taxi, it's a short jaunt to the main Parks Canada parking lot that accommodates the stream of visitors descending on Cape Spear each day. This is our starting point for what will be a four-hour hike. Even though it wasn't my idea, it could turn out to be a brilliant final leg of the tour.

The sky is clear and it's reasonably warm. One hopes for some natural wonder to astound them all.

'Ain't life grand?'

My new approach. As if everything is bloody marvelous with the world. As if all they have on their minds is this spectacular piece of geography. Nothing more. Relaxed and unguarded and impulsive.

'Alleluia!'

A very good start, Lula.

I turn to the lady who sleeps with *The Dictionary*. 'Maude, what's a Newfoundland term for *a good bit of fun*?'

'A soiree. Like the Kelligrew's Soiree.'

'Anything else?'

'A time.'

'Right on. A *time* in Newfoundland is a get-together, a party, a celebration.'

'We'll make a *time* of it,' says Maude.

'We'll make a *real* time of it! I'm pumped, b'ys. I'm really pumped!'

They don't know what to make of me. That's part of the strategy. Get them thinking they are dealing with someone not altogether in the ballpark, and they'll loosen up, let down their guard in a way they haven't done before. Start speaking loud to me like I've lost a few of my senses and am half-deaf to reality.

The parking lot leads to a circular, part wooden, part gravel walkway that will eventually take us to the newer, operational lighthouse, as opposed to a further path that leads to the original, museum-quality, defunct lighthouse.

'It will all make sense in the end.'

Do they believe me? It doesn't matter.

At various points the walkway branches off to lookout platforms that give a better view of the open ocean. They're there to encourage people not to wander off on their own and get too near the water's edge, as mainlanders tend to do when they see saltwater splashing on rocks.

'Attention, folks. Over the years there have been a total of eight people washed off these rocks by rogue waves. If you do dare Mother Nature and lose, rest assured that I will not be risking my own life in a fruitless effort to save yours.'

Nobody smiles. They're not meant to.

Then, as if the sea curling and spuming to shore weren't enough, there's a sudden sighting of the most renowned of all sea mammals. Maybe a hundred yards off shore.

Yet again the paradox that is Newfoundland saves the day. A humpback whale, as clear as its dorsal fin rising out of the water as it arcs and dives.

And then, about a minute later, with all eyes glued to the spot, a full-length breach—back arched, fins spread, a huge splash back onto the surface.

All four pairs of their eyes are practically socketless.

'Good God, man,' says Aiden, 'does it get any better than that?'

'What a time!' declares Maude. 'What a (quote-unquote) *time!*'

Maude has a sense of humour. It has taken something truly spectacular to bring it out.

'You wouldn't want to have that crawling in bed with you for the night!' says Lula. She lives in hope.

'*Merci, Sébastien*, for sharing your delightful province with us. We are blessed.'

Is she having second thoughts about kicking my dog?

'My pleasure.'

'Now all we need is to see a proper iceberg and our tour experience will be complete.'

Some people do take perverse pleasure in seeking the best of all possible worlds. I prefer to ignore such people and have their ungratefulness fester until it comes back to haunt them.

It doesn't take long. When we reach the head of the Cape, the point at which is erected a sign proclaiming 'The Most Easterly Point in North America,' there it is, in all its glory, just coming into view. The consummate iceberg.

No ifs, ands, or buts. Sun glinting off the magnificent specimen, calved months before from a glacier in western Greenland. An outrageously beautiful opening in its centre, giving the appearance of having been sculpted into a towering iceberg arch. The water around its base a remarkable translucent turquoise.

'There you have it, folks. One of creation's finest.'

Can they disagree? Not if they have any sense of fair play.

They can hardly believe that Newfoundland has pulled off the one-two punch, and so early in the hike. I could bask in it, I could turn momentarily smug, but no, I'll rise above pettiness and give the devil his due. It was luck, pure and simple. I will, however, hold off admitting that.

Once they have had their fill of iceberg and the final photo is taken and sent off to unsuspecting relatives, I remind them of where we are positioned. 'Think, my friends. As we stand here, whale to the left of us, iceberg to the right, we are the most easterly human beings on the whole of the continent. Every last other person is at our backs. If suddenly, continental drift were to reverse itself, we would be the very first people to step ashore in...in...'

Ireland? France? Spain?

'Africa. That's right. Africa. The eastern third of New-foundland was once joined to Africa.'

I could get carried away with this. It is a tour guide's prerogative to be painfully knowledgeable. I do pride myself on knowing when to stop, of allowing the client free association with the moment. I'm very aware of making time for them to absorb the cerebral Zen, as I like to think of it. Cameras tucked away, binoculars hanging at chests, deep breaths everyone.

As we stroll along the safe outer reaches of the path, I keep commentary to a minimum. And, as tempting as it is to fill in the complete historical record when we arrive at what's left of the WWII bunker, built to defend the entrance to St. John's Harbour, it being on the direct route of the trans-Atlantic convoys, I refrain. The ten-inch gun tends to speak for itself.

That and the interpretative storyboard. It has the additional advantage of being bilingual. Renée is bent over it, and appears to be quite intent. I can easily imagine that in another life she was in the French Resistance, or worked as an operative for French counter-espionage. I can picture her in a roguishly angled red beret and kerchief and black seamed nylons.

My imagination is getting the better of me, which I realize is entirely counter-productive. After the FedEx incident I should be looking for something vaguely sinister. If there is someone with something to hide it's Renée.

The trail continues. In places, it passes not far from steep drop-offs to grisly rocks below. Signs depicting a stick figure plunging headfirst to certain death add an element of déjà vu.

They seem to be paying it particularly close attention, thankfully. No one ventures near an edge. No one speaks the unspeakable.

I let it pass. The tactic is to build Renée's confidence that the cops have no suspicion of foul play. That they have no notion of Lois Ann hiding anything, and certainly that no one is suspecting her, Renée (thief that she is), of trying to cover up anything involving Lester. I am gaming for the big reveal, the slip-up that will clinch the fact that Renée Sipp is not who or what she is pretending to be.

It is a long climb up a series of wooden stairs to reach the base of the operational lighthouse, the most visible structure at Cape Spear. It's an octagonal concrete tower, bright white in the sunshine, rising some fifteen metres, and with a light that flashes three times every fifteen seconds. Off limits to visitors, as expected.

Lula needs a rest after the climb, and Renée needs a chance to expose her feet. She seems to have chosen perfectly good, low-cut hiking shoes, but nevertheless, she has the urge to take them off, together with her socks. She sits on a rock, massaging her feet and then stretching them forward, her red toes wriggling provocatively in the salt-air breeze.

The other two women look the other way, out of jealousy, if I am interpreting their facial expressions correctly. Renée's sexy foot display is for my benefit no doubt, although Aiden, the old dog, can't seem to turn his eyes away. Before Renée covers her feet again she extends each one forward to its very limit and holds the pose, in a declaration of the suppleness that extends to the rest of her being.

Aiden is consumed. I feel the urge to wink knowingly at him, but know better. Nor do I give Renée the least indication that I'm remembering where those feet have been in the recent past. Contrary to what she might assume, man does not live by lust alone. I'm feeling virtuous.

'Off we go then.' Up a moderate incline a hundred metres to the older lighthouse, restored to what it was in the late 1830s. It's a museum, and its beacon level offers a 360 degree view of Cape Spear and its rugged interplay of rock and the relentless North Atlantic.

It is here, perched on the far edge of the continent that you come to grips with your tenure on planet Earth. Incalculable at the best of times, here it seems even more precipitous. Overstep your boundaries and you might never live to regret it.

From here, looking north, Signal Hill can be easily spotted. My first thought is to avoid pointing it out, the sight of Lester's plunge, thinking nobody needs to be reminded.

I have second thoughts. I borrow Aiden's binoculars and focus them on the exact spot along the North Head Trail. I believe I can see the sun glinting off the chain handrail.

'Have a look, Renée. If the binoculars were more powerful, I bet you would still see the stain of Lester's blood on the rock.'

She is suddenly and unequivocally revolted. 'How cruel of you, *Sébastien*! Have you no *dignité*?' A definite overreaction.

She dismisses the offer of the binoculars with an exaggerated swipe of her hand.

I've touched a nerve. A very raw nerve.

The best course of action is to quietly withdraw my outstretched hand. Her Gallic temperament is clearly on the loose.

Well before the others have finished seeing all they want to see of the museum, Renée has exited the lighthouse, and gone to stand by herself against the white picket fence that runs between the lighthouse and the cliffs. I catch sight of her through one of the first-floor windows.

She's smoking. I've not seen her with a cigarette before. Smokers are rare on these tours, and when I do discover someone lighting up it is usually done covertly, running counter, as it does, to the ethos of the hiker.

While the others check out the gift shop, I step outside and join her. It is not what she wants, obviously. I sniff the air, hoping it is Gitanes she is smoking. It is something much more mundane. Nevertheless, I'm quick to share in her sins.

'I used to smoke. I still love the smell.'

'I don't.'

They all say that. They're all trying to quit.

'What are *your* dreams, Renée? Your ambitions?'

She remembers. I can afford to be bold. With only a few hours remaining and nothing to lose, I can. From what I know of the French they are all about being bold.

She turns to me. A forced smile penetrates the exhaling smoke. 'I drink wine. I paint. I travel.'

'And do you do them well?'

'I try.'

'Do you play to win?'

'Always.'

Where am I taking this? I honestly don't know.

Then she says, 'I wouldn't give up the life I have.'

'For love nor money?'

It elicits another forced smile, but nothing more.

She's a tight ship. As was *Titanic* before it sank, approximately 550 kilometres SSE from where we are standing.

Soon Lula arrives on the scene.

She is quieter than when we started out this morning. Her escapade of last night seems to have caught up with her.

'Are you going to be okay, Lula? We have a longish hike ahead of us.'

She nods. Nothing more. Very unlike Lula. Stories flash before me of hikers suffering heart attacks along the trail and having to be evacuated by orange-suited paramedics. I can't think that two client deaths would do much for the popularity of future tours.

Aiden and Maude arrive. They do nothing to increase the energy quotient.

Here I have it. A clientele consisting of four sluggish day-trippers about to set off on a four-hour hike. Which they brought on themselves! Which I'm tempted to remind them, but choose not to.

What is with these people? Are they thinking, after the stratospheric high of the whale and iceberg, that anything that follows can only be anticlimactic? Have they lost faith in the Newfoundland seascape to rouse and inspire? Or has fatigue, both physical and cultural, truly set in?

I'm not about to stand idly by and let it take hold. Time to pump things up, and firmly.

'First person to finish the hike gets their money refunded!' Expectant pause. 'Just kidding.'

The ten-kilometre hike from Cape Spear to Petty Harbour is but a small part of the East Coast Trail which traverses the jagged coastline of eastern Newfoundland.

We pick up the trail just past the lighthouse. It winds along a coastal ridge from Cape Spear, with terrific views of the cliffs as they notch their way south to the tip of the Avalon Peninsula. Much of the reddish sandstone path is through open barrens, its fresh green vegetation interrupted here and there by hunks of rounded rock, and occasionally by huge boulders. There are sometimes small streams or bog, with wild flowers to gladden the hearts of the multi-lensed photographer.

Toward its end, the trail turns slightly inland, through woods that offer a more secluded, rougher hike, though never is it anything more than moderately difficult. When it reemerges from the woods, the trail runs again near the cliffs, where it offers its most spectacular views, before coming to an end in the settlement of Maddox Cove.

Lula is my barometer. If at any time it is more than she can handle, then I'll have to slacken the pace, make more frequent rest stops. So far, so good. She seems to have shaken off her earlier doldrums and is moving along at a leisurely, but steady clip, her cane in full motion.

It's the fresh air. Newfoundland should bottle it up and sell it like oxygen. On a day like today, with patches of fog skirting the coastline, you can feel the molecules stroking your lungs. It's a pulmonary cleanse, ridding the air passages of the grunge of ordinary living.

I make the case to Renée, nonverbally. When she next looks my way I take a deep, lung-cleansing breath, and smile.

It only irritates her. 'Nothing more *suffisant* than an ex-smoker.' Sounds a lot like *insufferable*.

'*Pardon*, Renée.'

It's a fine line I'm trying to walk—keeping on her good side, while subtly poking, probing, working to get the wrong-doer to show through.

We stop from time to time to take in the seascape, to look back at the receding Cape Spear, noting how far we have come. It's important we shed ourselves of the urban reserve. Put the past behind us. Loosen up. Breathe.

I propose a series of deep-breathing exercises. We rid ourselves of all backpacks and walking devices.

'Everyone face the ocean. Hands free and hanging loose to your sides. Spines straight. Breathe deeply and hold. On the count of three. 1…2…3. Exhale. Feel the toxins being forced out. Feel the pure oxygen replacing them. Again. Breathe deeply. Hold. On the count of three. 1…2…3. Exhale.'

'You're faking, *Sébastien*. And this *merde* is slowing us down.'

It definitely crushes the moment. I've rubbed another nerve.

'We all have planes to catch.'

They've done the calculations, have they not? Back to hotel by 4. First flight at 6:30. Airport fifteen minutes away. Loads of time.

'We need to get moving,' insists Renée.

'I disagree,' says Lula. 'I'm quite enjoying this.'

Renewed friction within the ranks. To judge by the look Renée gives Lula, this could be intense.

Aiden steps in. He confirms the times with me then lays them out to Renée. It defuses her argument, but does nothing to lessen the tension that's now rampant between Renée and the other three.

I'm thinking, whoa, there's something major underlying all this. Something I know nothing about. Something that went on with Renée in the hotel room before I arrived.

I need to bait it out into the open. Force someone to crack under pressure.

It won't be Renée; she's got nerves of steel. But the other three are all possibilities.

'What will it be, folks? Another round?'

No response.

'Hands hanging loose. Spines straight.'

Renée walks away, pissed off.

'Breathe deeply and hold. On the count of three. 1…2…3. Exhale. Feel the toxins being forced out. Feel the pure oxygen replacing them. Again. Breathe deeply. Hold. On the count of three. 1…2…3. Exhale.'

We have lunch along a section of the trail called Empty Basket Cove. There's a good collection of rocks for sitting and there's general agreement that this is as comfortable a spot as we are likely to find. General, but not unanimous. No surprise.

In the end Renée sits and sulks her way through the choice of multi-grain sandwiches, fresh fruit-salad cups, and blood orange San Pellegrino.

I'm nothing if not civil. 'Renée, would you like dessert— *pain au chocolat.*' Looks like they were chosen with you in mind.

'I think not.'

'A half?'

'No.'

Where is the French fetish for politeness? Suddenly gone to the four winds.

We sit in silence. Fortunately, the view overlooking Empty Basket Cove is impressive by any standards. We can catch a glimpse of the stony beach at the base of the cliffs, and hear the rhythmic sweep of the waves over the stones and back again.

While the others all rave about it, Renée has decided to be blatantly blasé.

The woman looks preoccupied, ill at ease, as if there's something unpredictable ahead. Likely she's just decided to be a bigger pain in the butt.

'*Fantastique?*' I offer, looking seaward.

'Oh, give it up, *Sébastien*! You're driving us all crazy!'

There's a pause, until Lula turns to Renée and erupts. 'Oh, don't be such a crank!'

'And don't you be such a drunk.'

The gloves are off. Off and thrown over the cliff.

'Gawd, woman, how did you get to be so ornery? You're enough to make the devil depressed.'

'Now, folks,' says Aiden.

'Let's be civil,' says Maude.

'Fuck civil!' Between her teeth, but without the French accent.

There's sudden silence, except for the wash of the waves onshore. I take a deep breath. *On the Rock(s)* has had its moments. None quite like this one.

Renée is bursting to discharge once again, but is somehow managing to hold back. She retrieves a cigarette and lights it angrily.

While they all stew in silence, I gather up the remnants of lunch, seal them in a plastic bag and stuff the bag in my backpack. And with that I shoulder the backpack and move off.

'Lovely setting for a brawl.'

I hear grumblings behind me, but ignore them.

I walk until I'm well out of voice range, find a rock to sit on, until civility returns.

I can see they are still arguing among themselves. I'll wait them out.

It's just past noon. Nicholas should be out of school and on his way to check on Gaffer. I give him a call.

'What's up, pal?'

'Hey, Dad.'

He sounds good. Relief. I never know what I'm going to hear at the other end of the line.

'I've just turned on to your street.'

'Everything okay?'

'Yeah.'

'Your mother okay?'

'Yeah, I guess so.'

I'm tempted to ask about the third party, but figure it's best not to.

'Asshole is okay, too, I guess,' says Nick.

Somehow I didn't need that. 'Nick, man, you're going to have to come up with another name for him.'

'I can think of a few.'

'Maybe he's not as bad as you think.' I try not to choke.

No response.

I stay on the line until he's in the house. Until I hear the dog yelping in the background.

'I better go, Dad. Gaffer is going crazy.'

'Love ya.'

'Love ya, Dad.'

It's a bit of normalcy cutting into my otherwise abnormal world. I look back and see that the four of them have begun to walk in my direction. There's not much distance between them, which would suggest that they have somehow settled their differences. Will wonders never cease?

Not only that, but by the time they reach me they are chatting to each other, as if that awkward little dust-up had never taken place.

'Well, aren't we the happy lot.'

'We must apologize,' says Aiden. 'We put you in an awkward position.' Maude nods her head dutifully.

'Good manners went up the creek,' says Lula.

And finally, the primary pain speaks up. '*Je suis désolée, Sébastien.*'

I assume it's an apology. She looks contrite.

'As they say, what happens on tour, stays on tour.'

That takes a moment to kick in.

I should have learned by now to roll with the punches. The life of a tour operator is too short to get hung-up on personality clashes. They seem to have sorted out their differences, so let's move on and get the show back on the road.

Of course I'm keeping a close watch on Renée. She's definitely out of sorts, but maybe I'm barking up the wrong tree. Maybe she's had enough of dealing with other people, and she's just longing to get re-rooted back to her own soil, on her own terms. True enough, there is the matter of the stolen FedEx. Which reminds me that I should be giving Olsen a call.

It'll have to wait. We need to pick up the pace. I had thought of a side trek to North Head, a stubby peninsula that projects seaward just past Empty Basket Cove, but we'll have to forego that in favor of making up for lost time. The trail winds past it, never far from the coast, past Howlett's Cove, Cronnick's Cove, Killockstone Cove. Past vestiges of an abandoned community from the 19th century. There's little to show for its having been there except piles of foundation rocks.

We achieve a solid, relaxed rhythm, punctuated with brief stops to take in a particularly scenic ocean view, or to admire an unusual inland rock formation. Lula has been on the lookout for a pitcher plant, the provincial emblem, and sure enough a fine specimen shows itself in a particularly marshy bit just before we get to Herring Cove.

It is worth the stop. Lula insists on taking the photographs herself. She captures the leathery wine-red flower and its bulbous, pitcher-shaped leaves from every angle possible. Without her cane she's much less than sure-footed. I'm afraid she'll fall and not be able to right herself.

'The pitcher plant is carnivorous, as we all know.' All except Renée. An explanation is in order. Fortunately, I have this down pat. '*Sarracenia purpurea* captures insects that have fallen into the nectar and rainwater found at the base of these leaf structures. Bacteria and enzymes in the nectar break down the drowned insects, allowing the nutrients to then be absorbed into the plant's digestive system.'

'Wikipedia is a terrific resource,' says Maude. 'I read the same article.'

What a sweetheart. Someone should see if she can be cloned. I'll have her know I consulted a number of articles. And they weren't all Wikipedia.

Just past Herring Cove the trail veers inland and it is here that I detect a tightening of the ranks. They're feeling a need to negotiate the footpath more carefully, to help each other past any rough spots. There are two uphill climbs over uneven stones, in one case coupled with crossing a small stream. I cross first, then extend a helping hand to anyone who might wish it, pulling back the offer at the first sign of anyone who might take offence. Ageism, sexism, cynicism—they're all possibilities.

Weaving our way through a section of boreal forest has its own diversions. There's more life underfoot, more colour, especially the variation of mossy greens, strong vegetal whiffs of spruce, fir, juniper. It's a walk to ravish the unsuspecting senses.

I would prefer they slow down and take it all in, but they seem determined to get out the other side, as if they find it claustrophobic. They're a strange lot. Just when you think there would be something to satisfy them…

You're left flabbergasted.

Jesus. What's he doing here? The Latvian taxi-driver. The ex-basketball player, who is even taller now that he's no longer behind a steering wheel. He's dressed as if he's been running the trail.

None of the others are surprised to see him.

Aiden made arrangements to have him pick us up in Maddox Cove? He got there early, got bored and started walking in the path to meet us?

The others are strangely unresponsive, as if they expected it and now don't know what to make of it. I need an explanation.

'Ivo?' says Aiden.

That's his name? Ivo.

'Nobody,' says Ivo. 'The last—ten minutes ago.'

'Saw them,' says Aiden. 'A couple. Passed us.'

'Behind you?'

'Before we entered the woods. I checked. At least two kilo-metres and dawdling.'

What is this? A scouting report?

'Just in case,' says Ivo.

Aiden nods to Maude. She turns around and starts back the way we have just come. 'Just to where you get a clear view.'

A clear view of what? What the hell am I missing here?

I turn to Ivo, then back to Aiden. 'Would one of you mind expla…?'

'It's not you, *Sébastien*. It's your suspicions.' Renée, behind me.

Suspicions?

'You think one of us pushed Lester over the cliff.'

'You've been poking around for clues,' says Lula.

'You're not very subtle,' says Aiden. 'You wouldn't make much of a private eye.'

What the fuck?

'Fact is. . .' says Aiden, who hands Ivo an envelope, which he looks through quickly and stuffs in his jacket pocket.

'Fact is,' says Lula, 'Ivo makes a very good cabbie. And he likes to jog.'

It's a smack to the side of the brain. They're telling me Ivo was the jogger on the Signal Hill Trail?

They're telling me nothing. But Ivo is looking more serious by the second.

'Fact is,' says Aiden, 'you've finished your detective work. You're signing off.'

'His car keys,' says Lula.

'Hand them over,' Ivo tells me, his basketball-width hand outstretched.

'What use are they to you?'

'You'll never know. Not where you're going.'

'And what exactly does that mean,' I snap back indignantly. Suddenly it dawns on me what it could mean. Holy fuck.

I fish the keys out of my pocket and drop them in a noisy heap into his hand. His fingers curl back over them and they disappear into his own pocket.

What now? Ivo unzips his silver Nike running jacket and reaches one hand inside.

'No guns,' says Aiden.

Ivo slowly withdraws the hand. Basketball Boy has a hand-gun?

Or was he faking it to scare the shit out of me?

If so, he's succeeded.

Exactly what the hell do they have in mind? Whatever it is, it's not good. I look around, silently appealing for something. Anything. I don't know what. An explanation. An excuse. Laughter at falling for the gag.

Aiden is stiff, emotionless. He could be completing a bank transaction. He could be purchasing a new car, bargaining for options.

Lula looks taller, straighter, more firm on her feet. She's caneless, setting it against a tree, as if it were a prop. A prop no longer needed. She seems to have shed ten years.

Renée is behind me, but she won't escape my gaze, as much as she might wish to. She looks the most uncomfortable, the most vulnerable. What is it, Renée? Was all this in your mind when you were spread across my bed last night? Did you figure even then that you would do me in? Did you fake everything?

My eye catches hers for only a fraction of a second. She stares away, to something that doesn't need staring at. She's not herself, whatever that self might be. There's no knowing. Probably she's not even French. The fraud.

Ivo suddenly decides to get chummy. He plants himself next to me. Easier to latch those oversized paws of his on me should I decide to make a run for it.

'Let's get to it,' he says to Aiden. 'We shouldn't be wasting time.'

'Waste all the time you want.'

My lame diversionary tactic gets me nowhere, except further along the trail to whatever Basketball Boy has in his head. Lula is in the lead, I'm one step ahead of my tormenter, Aiden a few steps behind him. And Renée—who knows where.

'This won't take long,' he says to Aiden.

'Absolutely.'

What won't take long? And what's some nutcase from London, Ontario, agreeing to? Absolutely fuckin what?

Do I make a run for it? Only to get tackled and dragged to my feet again? I got about as much chance of getting away from six-foot-six Joggernuts with hands on him like a bloody grizzly as I do of winning the lottery. Which is zero since I never buy a ticket.

Better I should wait and see what's working through their screwed-up minds. Which doesn't take long.

We break out from the woods, go farther along the path and there it is. What's crowding their thick brains. A rock gorge dropping at least thirty metres, on the far side straight down a rock face to a mess of jagged boulders washed by the surf.

I can't believe it for a second. I can't let myself believe it because if I do I have no bloody hope of ever coming through this alive.

'You're kidding, right?' That's what I can manage. 'You're kidding?'

'Afraid not.'

Okay, let's get this straight. They are about to send me flying into the gorge because they figure I figure they hired Joggernuts to kill Lester. Not just one of them hired him like I thought. They all did. They were all in it together. Which doesn't make sense. They weren't going to get their money back from Lester. Revenge? It is just for revenge?

'You won't get away with it! The RNC will figure out I was with you. I don't show up. They come looking.'

'You left us at the end of the trail in Maddox Cove,' says Aiden. 'We got a cab to the hotel where we met Lois. Another cab to the airport. You started to walk back to Cape Spear to get your car which you left on the parking lot, thanks to Ivo.' Asshole Ivo holds up the keys.

'You got too close to the edge. You fell. It's tomorrow before anyone figures out you're missing. And who knows when they find your corpse. Maybe never. Maybe washed out to sea.'

'The cops are smarter than that. Who do you think I've been talking to?'

'Evidence, Sebastian? They have no evidence. And you're dead.'

'They have the FedEx.'

That gets Renée in the picture, and quick.

'I have the FedEx,' she says.

'You think you do. I took it from your room, Renée.'

'He's lying. I saw the envelope in my suitcase when I packed.'

'Empty.'

'He's lying.'

'Did you check it?' says Aiden to Renée.

'Empty!' I shout at him. 'The passport is in the hands of the RNC.'

'He's lying to save his skin.'

'How would I know it's a passport? The envelope was sealed

when you stole it. Not looking good, Renée. You won't like prison.'

'Enough of this bullshit!' shouts Ivo. 'We're wasting time! Some hiker shows up and we're screwed.'

I see Aiden getting frantic. Suddenly second guessing himself. It's Lula who jumps in.

'Let's move it.'

Ivo is behind me, shoving me towards the spot where the drop is the steepest.

'Hands off me you fucking asshole!'

He's not impressed. If there's any hope of coming out of this alive it's definitely not in following the sequence of events he has in his head.

I steel myself to make a sudden dash for it. Even the briefest jump on him and I'll get away from Joggernuts long enough to screw up his plans. I'm off like Usain Bolt on steroids. Get the hell out of the way, Lula, or get plowed under. I'm coming through!

Jesus. The next thing that hits me is the footpath. Square in the face. I look up and there's the buzzard Lula holding her cane in front of her like a lightsaber.

Joggernuts clamps his hand on the collar of my jacket and plants me on my feet. 'Try that again and you're a fucking dead man.'

He means sooner rather than later.

Here's where Ivo goes into high gear. It's not pretty.

'Fuck off with the choking.' Which squeaks out rather hopelessly, because he's doing exactly that—choking me, and with my own jacket, his grip on the collar so tight at the back of my neck that the zipper at the front is cutting into my windpipe.

'Get rid of his cellphone.' It's Lula. Her directive causing Joggernuts to release me from the choke hold, whether she intended it or not.

'Hand it over,' Ivo barks.

I'm in no hurry. If I have a lifeline the cellphone is it. If I somehow survive a thirty-metre drop onto jagged granite, the phone would be the one chance for rescue. Not great odds any way you chew it, but at this stage of the game I'm desperate.

I have one chance. That's it, one chance. People do survive long falls. Not many. But some do. I read about it. On the Internet. After Lester's crash.

We're not yet to the steepest part. From what I can see over the edge, it's not straight down. There's no way to stop a fall, but maybe there's a way to slow it down. That's what it said to do. Grab onto whatever you can, even if it snaps off. Aim for ledges. Keep your body loose. Bend your knees. Roll and tumble. Watch your head.

My one chance. And praying, I'll try that too.

'You want my phone! The hell you do!'

And with that I jump. Over the brink. Barely enough to slip past the edge and down!

There's no doubting it's down. It's not a plunge. Thank God, not a plunge. A brutal scrape of my lower back and buttocks over fist-sized rubble, upper body angled forward, outstretched arms that manage to grab a snarly piece of shrub, then another. The first uproots, the other snaps away. One foot catches a slab of rock poking through, propelling me sideways, and suddenly the length of me is rolling wildly—arms encasing my head—over a giant washboard of bedrock. Each ridge razing another bone, and tumbling faster still.

It ends on a ledge, one with no width to hold a body reeling at this speed. I peel over the edge of it, dropping several metres with a hefty thud onto gravel scree, long enough to right myself so I'm skidding feet first. Flailing, struggling in vain to dig in my heels. I can see the scree ends in a jumble of boulders, and just before crashing into it I manage to scrunch my limbs into a ball.

Like a body slammed onto concrete. My left hip gets the worst of it, and when I roll away from the rock, it's to drop another few metres , smacking flat on my other side.

I know nothing of what happened next.

Later—I don't know how much later—there's water, cold and lapping first at my hands, then head, my intact head.

My eyes open to wet beach pebbles. It is more the taste, of salt and water, and the sting of brine into the raw, broken skin of my hands.

I'm alive. That much I know. And I know I might never move. My body is a heap that has nothing of itself to give.

I'm flat on my stomach, my head and hands in the direction of the sea. Saltwater has risen to the level of my head. Higher with each successive wave.

It splashes against my head and reaches far enough that when it recedes it drains into my nostrils. The choice is to raise my head or breathe it in.

This is a clump of a body with the sense to move but not a whit of strength to do it.

There's a hell of a pain in my left thigh and hip. I think something must be broken. The right side tells me nothing and, if I could, I'd turn myself onto it.

My only choice is to do something to move myself away from the water. I haven't survived the fall only to give up and drown. Leave Nicholas with a dead father on his hands.

The strength I need most is in my right leg. From what I can see and feel of it, it's come through unbroken. That's a guess, for now.

The goal is to lift my right leg and press my foot into the beach pebbles with enough force to turn myself, gradually shift my body so my head is away from the water, not towards it.

The second I try to move, a god-awful thunderbolt jams through my left hip. My mouth jerks open with a grimacing screech and saltwater washes inside. I spit and cough and that makes it hell. Pure fuckin hell.

Okay, okay. Let's start again, before I get thinking it can't be done. Let's have another go with the leg before I bloody well drown.

Slowly, slowly. Teeth driving against each other. There's hellish pain, but it can't stop me. Centimetre by centimetre.

It takes me in the opposite direction from what I had in mind. No bloody difference. I'm moving. My head's veering away from the water.

Take a rest to let the pain subside, then go again. Rest and go. Rest and go. I gingerly work my elbows tight to my chest. Use them to lift my upper body. All the time turning, dragging. Slowly. Slowly working myself minutely inland.

I don't know how long it takes. An hour? Two? But eventually I'm far enough up the beach that only my feet are feeling the tide. If the tide rises more, I think I have beach enough to escape it.

I have no idea what time it is. At least it's still daylight. I've put off trying to retrieve my phone until I was out of the reach of the water. I wasn't ready for the disappointment of the phone being banged around so much it won't work.

It's in the right front pocket of my chinos. They got soaked and I'm thinking the cell fared even worse. I can feel where it implanted itself against my thigh. I sometimes put it in a waterproof pouch, if I know I'm going near water. Not today.

Getting my hand inside my pocket is hell. A teeth-gritting string of swear words does nothing to help, but at least my hand reaches the bloody thing. Now to ease it up and out. Sweet Jesus, I deserve a medal for not upgrading to something with a bigger screen.

It's in my hand in the open air, slowly making its way up to lie in front of my face. Up close and personal. And will it come alive after getting smacked to hell and back again? Will Apple come through when I could never possibly need it more than what I do right this second?

Fuck yes!! 6:47 lights the screen.

Yes Apple, you fuckin deserve your outrageous profit levels.

Of course it's the phone function that needs to work. There's some hesitation, as if I should be paying it more homage after being bounced off bedrock six ways to Sunday.

Just get me Olsen. One contact. That's all I need.

Yes.

'Olsen. Sebastian. Listen.'

'The passport. It turns out…'

'Listen.'

'But…'

'Olsen, shut up for fuck's sake!'

Silence. 'I'm at the bottom of a cliff. I just fell thirty goddamn metres.'

I exhale a mangled version of where I am and how I ended up there. He's impressed that I'm alive. And right away he's on another phone arranging a Coast Guard Rescue vessel to find me and pick me up.

'We got a couple of hours daylight. Anything broken?'

'Lots. Listen, you got to stop them at the airport before they board their flights. They were all in on it. I'll explain later.'

'Lois was discharged from the hospital.'

'She'll be there, too. And what about Joggernuts?'

'Who?'

'The taxi-driver, the Latvian jogger guy they hired, the asshole who was about to push me over the cliff.'

'No clue.'

'When you arrest them…'

'Question them. At this point that's all we can do. Detain them for questioning.'

'They were about to kill me.'

'First we have to decide if there is enough evidence to press charges. Did anybody push you? You said you jumped.'

'In self-defense.'

It doesn't get any response. He's gone then. I'm assuming to the airport, leaving me a fractured lump fuming on the beach. At least the tide is not pouring into my goddamn nose.

In the meantime I wait. And wait.

I'm deciding if I should call Nicholas. I don't want him to freak out. I'll be taken straight to the hospital and have God knows what done to me. Better hearing it from me than Olsen. Then there's Gaffer. Someone will have to check on the mutt.

'Nicholas, c'mon, man, answer your phone.'

It rings and rings. Nothing. It's forever before there's a voice at the other end.

'Sebastian.'

His mother's voice. 'Samantha?'

'Where the hell have you been?'

Exactly what you want to hear after careening down the side of a cliff, lying like a piece of shit, half dead.

When I don't answer right away, she hits me with both barrels. 'Do you even care what happened to your son?! He was in your house.'

'What are you talking about?'

'He got violently stomach sick from something he drank in your house! He calls you and calls you. No bloody answer. Where the hell were you?'

I don't bother.

'Is he okay?'

'After I took him to emergency.'

'What was it he drank?'

'Scotch.'

'Scotch!'

'He swears he only took a taste. The doctor says there must have been something else in it. Some substance. What the hell goes on in your house, Sebastian?'

Jesus. 'I'll find out.'

'You'll find out. Is that all you got to say?'

'As a matter of fact, no.'

Out floods the story of where I am and how I got there.

'Oh, my God.' Several times, progressively more subdued.

Before I tell her to give Nicholas a hug from me and I hang up, I detect genuine sympathy. That's refreshing.

I'm still waiting. The light is fading and it's turning colder. Maybe it's numbing the pain. I don't know anymore.

6

THERE'S NOTHING MORE helpless than lying in a hospital bed buggered up, going nowhere. Pumped up on pain killers, swarming with questions, desperate to get answers. Compression pump on the leg. Catheter up the dick. Inert.

Nurse Amanda offers no sympathy. 'Patience, Mr. Synard. You need rest. Your body needs time to repair itself. I'm sure you're thankful just to be alive.'

As it turns out she's someone I taught in high school, sounding more mature and efficient than I remember. She reveals that I 'turned her on to history.' Wonderful. I've had a private word with the male resident who checks on me from time to time to the effect that Nurse Amanda, ex-student, will not be the one to examine the catheter should it need examining.

'You've come though the operation so well,' says Amanda. 'The doctors are very impressed.'

It took a four-hour operation to repair the smash up on my hip. An *intertrochanteric hip fracture*, as the surgeon informed me after the MRI. Which is good, apparently. Meaning the hip joint itself came through the fall in decent shape. The fracture was between the trochanters, the nobby bits on the femur. And it is a *stable* intertrochanteric fracture. In luck again.

A nail was inserted down the canal of the femur, and then a lag screw through the nail and up and into the neck and socket of the bone. Sounds to me like the surgeon should be doing carpentry on his days off.

Of course I am as impressed as the docs were. I came through vertical hell with nothing else broken. Badly bruised but not broken. Head intact. Face intact, if looking like hell and still swollen. I'm inwardly rejoicing. I'm just not one to show it to Nurse Amanda, who knows better than I do what lies under the blanket, and if the truth were told likely had dealings with it prior to my coming out of anesthetic. Thankfully I'm in a private room.

You learn to put these things aside when you are in the hospital. Eventually. My mind is racing with everything that's happened that I don't know about. The first non-medical person to come through the door is Nicholas. Followed by his mother. They've come early, before school. With an overnight bag of my clothes.

'Nick, pal.'

'Dad. Holy crap, you look awful. Are you okay?'

'I'm good.'

'Oh, my God,' says Samantha, staring at me, a hand to her mouth. 'What are the doctors saying?'

'I'll recover. It'll take time.'

'I can't believe you did that. You're incredible.'

I could have used that adjective, say, five years ago.

'We've taken the dog home with us,' she says.

'I'll take good care of him,' says Nick.

'But you, man, what the heck happened?'

'I'm okay.'

'Fred had the lab analyze the Scotch. There were traces of disulfiram.'

'What the frig's disulfiram?'

'What alcoholics use to keep off the booze. It's a pill. They take it and if they drink alcohol it makes them violently ill. Headache, stomach sick…'

'I threw up my lunch all over your carpet.'

'And what the frig were you doing drinking Scotch?'

'I just wanted to try it. You love it so much, I figured it had to be good. I only had a couple of sips.'

'How did the drug get in there, Sebastian? That's the question.'

'Some idiot slipped it in the bottle, obviously.'

And there's only one person it could have been. Someone who wanted me out of the picture for the rest of the day. Someone who was surprised as hell when I showed up at the Delta later that morning. Someone who then had to make other plans when she discovered I hadn't drunk the Scotch like she had assumed I would.

I can't tell Samantha any of this.

When it does come out is when Olsen shows up, a half-hour after they leave. Before that Nurse Amanda arrives to change the catheter bag.

'We need to replace the night bag with the day bag.'

'I prefer…'

'Don't worry, Mr. Synard. I don't have to go anywhere near the penis.'

She can sound so professional.

'There's a valve partway down your leg.'

'Of course there is.'

I lie back, and let her do her job. I stare at the ceiling, thankful that I'm constipated. And that by tomorrow I will be allowed out of bed.

Olsen catches me asleep.

'Christ.' There's a pause while my eyes pop open. 'At least you're alive.'

Flat on my back is not how I want to be interacting with Olsen. Press a button and the head of the bed begins to tilt up. It doesn't go far before the hip takes notice. The eye-to-eye angle is better. Not great, but better.

'You sure as hell did the job on yourself.'

'Thanks.' Cops can be so observant. 'It was all in the timing.'

I can't be too hard on him. He did get the rescue squad to me in crack time.

'Surgery went well?'

Enough with the preliminaries. We both know what we need to talk about.

We start with the passport. It does belong to Lester's wife. The cops have no clue who sent it to him. They had a search warrant to go through Renée's luggage. No FedEx envelope.

'She must have garbaged it when she got back to the hotel.'

'Which means,' he says, 'there's no evidence she ever had it.'

'I took it from her suitcase!'

'Exactly. A lawyer would have a field day. In any case we know it was sent from Paris, right?'

'That's what it said.'

'Any sender name and address would probably be fake. In any case we're getting FedEx to check their records.'

'It was Renée who drugged the Scotch.'

To which I have to add a measured amount of detail.

'Interesting. I wish I had known this before.'

Apparently, after the results of the lab test Samantha poured the rest of the Scotch down the sink and rinsed out the bottle. In which case she would have washed out the two glasses. Cleaning one of lipstick.

To Olsen's credit he doesn't poke his nose where it shouldn't go. But yes, Inspector, I am not without a sex life. Torrid, on occasion.

'The real question is why was Lester sent his wife's

passport? And why would Renée not want you to know he had it?'

'Put the question to her, make her confess. Isn't that what you guys are good at?'

Olsen looks at his watch. 'Any minute now she should be landing.'

'What are you talking about?'

'Her plane should be just about to touch down?'

'Her plane?'

'In Paris.'

Jesus.

According to Olsen the RNC had no goddamn evidence to lay charges. The five of them were each questioned separately at the airport. They all had the same story, except for Lois, who didn't need a story. They all contended that when they finished the hike in Maddox Cove they called a taxi that took them to the Delta, where they met Lois, got their luggage and took another taxi to the airport. While I turned around and walked the trail in reverse, back to Cape Spear, to pick up my car and drive home. Tour ended. Except for me not watching where I was going, losing my footing, and plunging over the cliff. They even suggested that I might have been distracted by my cell phone.

'They all said to tell you how happy they are that you're alive.'

'Bloody liars!'

I'm beyond furious. Beyond furious and an inert lump in the bed. My only vent is my mouth and it vents for a very long time.

Olsen waits me out.

'The fact is, Synard, there was nothing we could do. You

jumped. You said that yourself. Plus, we have nothing substantial to link them to Lester's death. Plenty of speculation, but nothing substantial. If there comes a point we have the evidence, they'll be brought back to face charges. Including Renée and Lula. Canada has extradition treaties with both countries.'

Cold comfort. It seems to me they were allowed to slip away like bloody snakes. 'All five of them should be in the lock-up living on stale bread and water.'

Olsen chuckles. Okay, so I haven't lost my sense of humour. I can even force a return smile.

'Sebastian, rest up, get back your strength. This is not over yet. There's one person we haven't questioned.'

'Joggernuts.'

'Not how I refer to him, but yes, the jogging taxi driver. The one person we can charge—assault, car theft—if we find him.'

'It shouldn't be hard. There ain't exactly many oversized Latvians roaming around the streets of St. John's.'

'You really think he's Latvian? Just because he told you he was Latvian?'

'You mean he lied?' The second it exits my mouth I realize how dumb it sounds.

'It's like a scar across the face. That's all you see.'

Okay, I get the picture.

'What colour was his hair?'

I say it again. 'I get the picture.' Out loud this time. 'Dark. His hair was dark. He was wearing a baseball cap.'

'Was there anything written on it?'

'As a matter of fact, yes. The print was small.'

'But you managed to get every word.'

'*Heaven is where all chefs are Latvian.*'

I overlook the fact that he laughs. I did, too. At the time.

'I asked him if he liked to cook. He said yes.'

'And you believed him?'

'I'm just saying he could be working in some restaurant around town.'

'And I'm saying he's very good at making himself look like something he's not.' He adds, 'You have to think like a cop.'

Do I now? Thank you, Olsen, for valuing my opinions. The next time I'll make a point of smashing both hips so you can feel even more superior.

'He's still tall and skinny and that sure as hell won't change.'

'And that's our best lead in tracking him down.'

'Unless he's been eating like hell since yesterday, bulking up hand over fist. Or in the hospital as we speak, getting several inches cut from each leg.'

Olsen smiles, self-boosting his ego. He leaves while he thinks he's ahead.

There's a good turn of phrase that used to be common in rural Newfoundland to describe someone puffed up with pride. *He's too big in his self.* Olsen is too big in his self. That about sums him up. I'd like to think Samantha had better taste in men. She did, at one time.

Self-pity? On my part? Really? Come to think of it, there hasn't been a time in my life—pulverized, hospitalized, catheterized, immobilized—when it would be more in order.

It's not self-pity. The doctors want me out of bed by tomorrow. So I won't seize up. Out of bed and into the armchair that's near the bed, walking with crutches the next day, home maybe the day after that. Several in-home visits from a physio-therapist. Then a regime of physio at an outpatient clinic.

'We are talking months to complete recovery, Mr. Synard.' Nurse Amanda likes to meet challenges realistically and straight on and expects others to do the same. She has a tight grip on me on one side, while Calvin, a brick of a male orderly, supports me on the operation side. We are making our way from The Comfy Chair to the toilet. Once there and they have deposited me, Nurse Amanda has the good sense to move off before further exposure takes place, not that the johnny coat hasn't made a half-naked fool of me already.

'I'm good, Calvin. Please close the door when you leave. I'll press the call button when I'm ready for pick-up. Cheers.'

I'm not particularly good. I'm in pain. But I'm determined as hell to get something done. Forty-five minutes later (after several 'just checking' inquiries from Amanda outside the bathroom door) I'm back in bed, defeated. Bowels on strike and refusing to bargain.

Simple bodily functions have taken over my life. I need a Scotch.

It gets better. By day three I am moving about on crutches. Up and down the hospital corridor, in the paisley silk lounge robe that Samantha dug out of my closet when there was a plain, perfectly good, cotton bathrobe she could have chosen. She was making a statement, the exact crux of which I'm not certain. In any case, my sheer tenacity gathers admiration from all quarters. I'm determined to be a quick healer, and pain will be no deterrent.

'Be careful not to overdo it, Mr. Synard,' Nurse Amanda warns. 'The body needs its rest if it's going to restore itself.' Out of the mouths of babes. I'm so exhausted that it takes her and Calvin to get me back in bed and properly aligned. I don't ask whose hand it is that came to rest on my bare buttock, if just briefly and likely with indifference.

I sleep, much more than usual. Sleep is good. 'Nature's healer, Mr. Synard.'

When I next hear from Olsen I'm in a better frame of

mind. I'm past the trauma and have entered the recovery phase. Which may account for the fact that Olsen is not half the pain in the ass he was on the first visit.

He's not brimming with good news, but there has been 'steady progress.' It's a euphemism for 'we're getting somewhere, it's just taking time.' Sounds like my lower intestinal function.

'A neighbour of yours saw a tall, thin young man get into your car and drive it away. He thought it odd at the time, especially since the guy was so tall he had trouble fitting in the driver's seat. But the guy had a key and it was obvious he wasn't breaking into the vehicle. It was late in the afternoon, which would have been about right. He says the guy was walking from farther up the street, at least as far as the convenience store. Which suggests he parked the van somewhere nearby, after he dropped the others at the Delta.'

'Ivo. The guy's name is Ivo.'

'We'll call him Ivo for now.'

Right. Until his real, non-Latvian name shows up.

'Once he left the car at the Cape Spear lot, *Ivo* likely got rid of the keys. Then he had to have a way of getting back to St. John's. He would have had to get someone he knew to pick him up, a friend, a relative, someone who could be paid to keep his mouth shut. Either using the van, or using another vehicle and returning Ivo to the van once they got back in town.'

'He looked like an Ivo.'

No reaction. He is still lacking a sense of humour.

'Do you remember the colour of the van? It obviously didn't belong to any of the cab companies. He would have parked outside the Delta that morning, waiting for everyone to come out.'

'I think it was yellow.'

'That makes sense.' Doesn't crack a smile.

'I seem to remember a meter.'

'Seem?'

'I wasn't sitting up front. And I didn't pay.'

He looks at me as if something doesn't add up. Like I was soaking clients for costs that should have been part of the tour.

'They insisted. I told you before that the hike wasn't on the schedule.'

'What make was the vehicle?'

'I don't know. I'm not into that sort of thing. It was a van—room for seven, including the driver. It was yellow. Not a bright yellow. There can't be that many yellow vans around town.'

'Lots probably, including the one which just got a new paint job and is no longer yellow. And had its meter taken out, if it had a meter.'

'You're giving Ivo way too much credit. He didn't look that smart.'

Olsen stares at me, holds it in. I am obviously not thinking like a cop. He doesn't say it. Which doesn't make it much better.

'Listen, Inspector. Say you were Ivo. You know the cops are looking for you. You know you stand out like a sore thumb because your head is permanently in the clouds in more ways than one. Wouldn't you try to skip town?'

'Maybe. Unless there was something keeping you here. A girlfriend?'

'Assault with intent to kill or a girlfriend, which would you choose? C'mon.'

'What if you didn't get paid. What if they refused to pay because Ivo didn't get the job done?'

'He got some dough. If he pushed Lester over the cliff, he did. If he did the fake job on Lois. Remember, sending me over the edge was a last minute scenario. They only came up with that after I showed up at the Delta. So it was add-on pay. I saw Aiden pass him an envelope when he first showed up on the trail. A wad of bills I figure. But then I buggered up their game plan. So he drops the five of them back to the hotel, expecting to keep some of the dough. Maybe not the whole shot, but a good chunk of change nevertheless.'

'They press him to hand back more of the money. What can he do?'

'He still has to drive the car to Cape Spear, remember, to make the story add up. He knows and they know their story has to add up. They're screwed if it doesn't. And he's screwed worse than they are because he's the one who could be charged.'

'Right.'

Which is Olsen's way of saying that now I'm thinking like a cop.

'Backtrack,' Olsen says. 'It was a last minute scheme so Ivo has to get his hands on a van and quick. Not very likely he had one of his own. So he has to borrow one for the day. Who does he go to? He's not got many choices. But he finds someone and swings a deal. Unfortunately the bugger's yellow. So then, after he messes up on the trail, he's worried. They're all worried. What if somehow the son-of-a-bitch survived. The van's too easy to track down. Guess who gets a phone call from the airport before they all fly away? Ivo. We think the guy's still alive. Get the hell out of sight. And, by the way, get that bloody van painted.'

'Chances are, even if Ivo's skipped town, whoever owns the van hasn't.'

'So someone in St. John's with a newly painted van knows something.'

This is taking cop logic to a whole new level.

I'm getting off on this. And Olsen knows it. Once he leaves the hospital room to get back to the station I'm left cursing the fact that I can't be out there doing something to track down the bastard hired to kill me, Latvian or bloody not.

Instead I'm propped up in a hospital bed, diligently healing.

Which, I suspect, Olsen is just fine with since I'm not getting in the way of his job. While, at the same time, he can play at being a stud in the house whose mortgage I slaved for years to help pay off, in the house I painted and wall-papered and landscaped. Where once I stood, now stands the stud.

There's an inner voice blaring.

Let it go, Synard, let it go. You're sounding like such a lameass.

Not long after Olsen exits, Samantha and son enter. Good timing. I would not have appreciated the three of them standing at the foot of the bed at the same time.

'Sebastian, you're looking a lot better. You're not so swollen.'

'I try not to look in the mirror.'

'You could wear sunglasses to cover the two black eyes,' says Nick. 'It could look very cool.'

You raise them up and they bite you in the butt any chance they get. 'Thanks, pal.'

He gives me the male-to-male nod. We have a good laugh. I love that kid.

'Okay folks, now for the good news. I can walk with crutches!'

Nick pumps the air with his fist.

'I went up and down the corridor today at least a dozen times. Tomorrow morning I get the catheter out. Tomorrow afternoon I think I should be able to go home!'

'What's a catheter?'

'Don't tell him. He doesn't need to know.'

'How do you spell that?' He's got his iPhone out ready to Google.

'Don't spell it for him.'

'Got it.' He always was a good speller. 'Is it a *ur-in-ary* catheter? Oh my God, Wikipedia has a picture and everything. Oh my God, that's not his…' He turns off the phone and puts it back in his pocket.

Samantha is laughing out loud. Nick is playing it for all it's worth.

'Give it up.'

'You let them do that to you?'

'Give it up!'

Nick shields his groin with his hands in mock pain. He bends over laughing.

Now he's got me laughing and it hurts like hell. Not just where my leg has been sutured, or my chest which is still sore from the crash and tumble down the cliff. It hurts in my heart because it reminds me of so many other times when the three of us had such a good laugh, about something or other. It doesn't matter what.

Day Four in the Health Sciences. Nurse Amanda still on duty. The last day of her shift. If the planets are properly aligned and all goes according to plan—my plan at least—it will also be the last day of my shift, and I'll be heading back to the old homestead on Military Road. There's an unopened bottle of Scotch awaiting. Samantha has offered to drive me.

Around ten o'clock the good doc arrives and authorizes the removal of said object. The procedure is a bit ticklish (i.e. delicate), but goes ahead without incident. No psychological residue. Nurse Amanda was not present.

But she can't help commenting the next time I hobble out of the bathroom. 'Everything back to normal?'

'Yes, everything's well in hand.' The double entendre only struck me after the fact, but didn't strike Nurse Amanda at all.

Nobody laughs. Which is a shame, I guess.

From here on in it's a matter of wait and see, killing time until the surgeon shows up and does his assessment. In the meantime I do several circuits of the corridor, resting in The Comfy Chair in between. *Nobody expects The Spanish Inquisition!* Always loved Monty Python.

Bored waiting. Another lap of the corridor. More chair time. Torture. I don't want the doctor showing up with me in bed. I want to look eager and fit. Even if it is torture.

It's after five before he finally makes his rounds. 'Now Mr. Synard, and how are we today?'

'Dandy.'

He's skeptical. 'Been up around and walking I hear.'

'Absolutely.'

'Very good. How about we get you in your bed so I can do a proper examination.'

I have no choice. And no choice but to get assistance. Nurse Amanda and Calvin do their respective duties (with considerable help on my part I will add) and I'm in bed and sitting pretty.

'Catheter removed I see. No worse for wear?'

'No, doctor. Everything's well in hand.' It flies past him as well.

He's too busy having a look-see at the sutured hip and thigh.

'Ummm. Healing nicely. A little bit redder than I would like it. Maybe a bit stressed from all that walking. I'm thinking one more day in hospital wouldn't hurt. Just to be on the safe side. A little more bed rest, Mr. Synard, a little less time on your feet impressing the nurses.

You can't win for losing! Can you? *Nobody expects The Spanish bloody Inquisition!*

The next day, promptly at 6 in the afternoon, Samantha and Nick are back. I'm dressed and in The Comfy Chair, crutches at the ready, overnight bag fully zippered and set to go. The surgeon has given his blessing, the release papers have been signed. My wallet is still intact. I have sung the praises of Medicare, several times.

Getting into the car is awkward, getting out even more awkward. It's like I have a vestigial appendage that's due for reactivation at some indefinite point in the future.

Nevertheless it's monumental to be home, alive if not kicking. Five days ago I was at the bottom of a cliff, half dead, and in danger of losing out to the other half. At this hour I'm lying on the couch in my living room, staring despondently at the best Islay Scotch in my beverage cabinet. I have been told not to mix alcohol with the pills I'm taking to dull the pain of having my leg nailed to my hip. Survival could be a lot worse. I guess.

Samantha was super. She has stocked my refrigerator and freezer with easy-to-cook meals, enough for several days. She made the bed in the downstairs spare room and stocked it with some of my clothes, so I won't have to climb the stairs. She's been all-around thoughtful and caring. I should break bones more often.

Nick wanted to stay over so he could be my go-to man if I need anything. I put him off so his mother didn't have to play the bad guy. Next weekend, I told him. You and Gaffer and me, together again, the whole weekend.

When they headed out the door, the front door closing behind them, there was a sadness hanging off the 'good-night and see you tomorrow.' He came very close to losing me. How much hurt that would have caused him.

Eventually I doze off and wake up in time to get ready for bed. A survey of the beverage cabinet reveals three bottles of whisky that have been opened but not finished. Am I willing to take the chance that loveable Renée didn't drop any surprises in those bottles as well? I suspect she wouldn't have had time. But I can't be sure. In the end I dump what's left of all three bottles, including the two-thirds-full Scallywag, down the kitchen sink and drop the empty bottles in the trash bin. The whisky gods moan.

I don't sleep well. I can only lie on my back, which drives me nuts because I end up snoring and snorting and waking myself up. Eventually I crutch my way back to the living room and pile into the La-Z-Boy, reclining as far back as the chair will go. Bundled up in a blanket, legs elevated, looking and feeling like a castoff from a nursing home.

Above and beyond all that, the restlessness comes from the itch to get on with it. *It* being playing Synard, untrained, unlicensed PI. Figuring out what became of Joggernuts and what clues he might have left behind. Figuring out how to serve up justice to the sociopaths who were planning to leave my kid fatherless.

It's not as if Olsen has any wish for me to do anything but stay out of the picture and let the RNC take care of business. In any case he must figure, given I'm a semi-invalid, I have zero choice in the matter. Let's not underestimate the incapacitated.

My watch is in my face. 4:17. Not yet daylight. It's a key I heard, in the front door.

I have no idea who it could be. Not Nick, surely to God, not at this hour.

'Nick? Samantha? My phone must be turned off.'

No answer. I feel a quick buzz of panic.

'Who is it?' And again, louder.

Still nothing. There's someone in the porch.

'Answer me.' Close to yelling it.

The knob on the door between the porch and the hallway turns. The chair where I'm sitting doesn't have a direct sightline to the door. I have to wait until someone breaks into view. I tilt the chair to its upright position. I switch on the lamp that sits on the end table next to me. It's all I can do, except shit my pants since I just thought about the set of keys that I last saw being tightened into a mammoth hand.

Sweet Jesus. Why did everyone automatically assume he had thrown them away?

The eyes that meet mine are Ivo's. Mine like an owl's, his an intensely solemn Latvian blue.

I'm thinking he has a gun. There is none, for me to see. He wouldn't need one, not with that pair of paws.

'You look okay,' he says. 'Never thought you'd live through that.'

He's cold sober. Unsmiling, motionless.

Pitiful, if I didn't know better.

'You break into my house in the middle of the goddamn night…'

'I didn't figure you'd be in any shape to come to the door.'

'What the fuck.'

'We need to talk.'

I'm in no position to argue.

'Can I come in now?' A squeak of a voice from the porch.

A girl, no more than twenty, wanders into view. She's wearing a low-cut halter top and over it an open sweater that reaches past her very short shorts. Her hair is a dark blonde loose mane of curls. Her head reaches Ivo's shoulder, which she is leaning against.

'This is Ashley.' She looks like an Ashley.

'Hi,' she says.

What else is there to do. 'Hi.'

'This is Ashley's idea. I think I'm royally fucked, but she thinks there's a chance.'

'Of what?'

'Of you believing I wouldn't have killed you.'

'Nice.'

'He wouldn't have,' says the girl. 'Ivo would never kill anyone. He might try to scare them, but he wouldn't kill them.'

An innocence that could be adorable, if it weren't so fucking ridiculous.

'They hired you to throw me over that cliff and now you're telling me you goddamn faked it. You were forcing me to the bloody steepest part!'

'I still wouldn't have done it. I was only out to scare you, so they would think I was going to do it.'

'So I jumped for no reason.'

'You might say that.'

'Bullshit!'

'Ash,' says Ivo. 'I told you what would happen.'

Ash is not buying it. 'It's true. We needed the money, that was all. He got a quarter up front and that was enough. The rest wasn't worth it.'

I'm not about to ask what it was worth to them to have me a quarter of the way bumped off.

'You pushed Lester over the cliff. Didn't you make enough money off that?'

'No way, man. I didn't push that guy over no cliff. They hired me to run the trail. They told me they wanted him distracted, that was all. I didn't know what they had in their minds. They were paying good money. Someone else pushed him. It wasn't me. I didn't even know it was going to happen.'

'Who?'

'The old lady with the cane? She was the closest to him. I didn't see it. I was past them when it happened. I could hear him cursing me for running so close to him.'

'So you're an accessory to a murder.'

'I told you I didn't know that's what they had in their minds.'

'A jury is not going to see it that way.'

'Fuck.'

'Don't swear, Ivo. You said you wouldn't swear.'

'Fuck.'

'You knocked down the other woman, around the lake. That was you.'

'I didn't hurt her.'

'In deeper all the time, Ivo. What were you thinking? Third time lucky?'

'It was big money this time. Me and Ash want to go to Latvia and get a place of our own. The quarter was going to be enough to do it.'

'My life was a starter home in Latvia?'

'I told you I wasn't going to kill you. But then you jumped and screwed up everything. I was going to hand you back your keys and you would have called the cops and they would have been arrested. But you screwed things up.'

'What's more, you're not even Latvian!'

'He is so Latvian! He speaks it and everything!'

'When I was going to school I worked on weekends in a restaurant in Liepāja, washing dishes. I want to become a chef.'

'He could become the Jamie Oliver of Latvia if he got some training.'

'Let me get this straight. You pull me back from the goddamn brink. So what would have stopped the others from turning on me?'

'Old age.'

He has a point. 'So I show up in Maddox Cave and call the cops. What charges are they going to lay on them? Intent to kill? I don't think so. They didn't lay a finger on me. It was all you. If there was anyone that was going to be arrested it would have been you.'

'And I would have been long gone.'

'Like they figure you are now.'

'That's why you got to believe me.'

'We talked it over,' says Ashley. 'Ivo would be willing to give himself up to the cops, but you got to help us convince the cops his story is true.'

'I don't have to do anything.'

'He's right,' says Ivo to the girl. 'Like I said, we're screwed.'

'Where's the money?'

'Western Union,' says Ash. 'Ivo sent it to Latvia. His mother is holding it for us. She's looking around for an apartment for us to buy.'

'In Liepāja,' says Ivo.

'Ivo tells me I'll like Liepāja,' says the girl. 'It's on the ocean, like St. John's, except it has a beautiful beach.'

'It's windy, like St. John's,' says Ivo.

'I don't mind wind.'

'And chilly in summer sometimes.'

'Tell me about it,' she says.

I don't believe it. I don't believe it. The fucking weather in Latvia. What planet are they on?

'Get serious. You won't be going to Latvia anytime soon. And if you try to make a run for it...'

'We know, the yellow van, a dead giveaway. I made a deal with a guy who I heard had a van he was selling. Let me borrow the van for the day, I told him, and if it works out, I'll buy it off you. That's what happened. Except it turned out to be yellow.'

'Yellow sucks,' says Ashley.

I don't ask where it is now. I don't ask why they haven't got it painted. I'm tired and my leg hurts and I want this to be over.

'Will you be on our side?' Ashley pleads.

'There's no sides to it, Ashley. There's Ivo and the cops and the truth. And, from what I know, turning himself in would help. The apartment in Latvia might have to wait.'

'We'll think about it,' says Ivo.

'I wouldn't think too long. Two o'clock this afternoon. Here. There'll be one cop.'

As they're about to go through the door, daylight is breaking.

'Ivo.'

He hands me the keys.

'Ivo.'

He looks back.

'You play much basketball growing up?'

'I hated basketball. Hockey. I love hockey. That's why I came to Canada. Sandis Ozoliņš is my God.'

Not to mix sports metaphors, but you know when life throws you a curve ball, then another, and another, you start to wonder, shouldn't I just hang up the cleats? Go sit on the bench and stay there?

I'm not noted for drinking Scotch at 10 in the morning, but I've eased off the pills in favour of a more appetizing pain management regime. True, it does prove a bit embarrassing when the overweight Ms. Thurber, physiotherapist, comes knocking. She can forgive me still in pajamas, but questions the uncorked bottle of Laphroaig on the end table.

'Laphroaig is noted for its medicinal qualities. Would you like to make your own judgment?'

'I'm afraid not, Mr. Synard.'

I should be more kind. She is doing her best. She settles herself on the couch opposite, sitting a bit forward, with her clipboard on her lap. 'Let's start with a few general questions about your comfort and safety.'

'Absolutely.'

Walking with crutches—no problem. Standing up from seated position—perfect. Getting in and out of bed—slow but entirely doable. Up and down stairs—tomorrow's project.

'How about your toilet functions, Mr. Synard. I understand you had a…'

'Yes, removed and everything back to normal.' A quick end to any c-talk.

'And what about bowel movement?'

'Moving along.'

'Have you thought about getting a raised toilet seat? Some patients find it puts less pressure on the hip.'

'I prefer to hover.'

'I beg your pardon.'

'Case closed, Ms. Thurber.'

There's a quick detour into my exercise agenda. Into ankle pumps, quad sets, heel slides, and gluteal sets, otherwise known as buttock squeezes. I'm on my back on the carpet, while she's on her knees adjusting the limbs as needed.

'Remember, Mr. Synard, take your time. Slow and steady is much better than rush, rush, rush. Slow, deep breathing throughout. I suggest three times a day, ten repetitions each to start, gradually working up to twenty. Restful music might help. Bach perhaps, Mozart. Many of my clients find great pleasure in some of Schumann's harpsichord pieces.'

'I'll make a note of that.'

'And please, Mr. Synard, no alcohol. It gives you a false sense of security, and we wouldn't want that.'

'Of course not.'

'Let me see you get up off the carpet on your own. Very important, of course. We wouldn't want you down and not be able to get up.'

'That would be a catastrophe of sorts.'

'Now, remember, no pressure on the knee of your healing leg.'

'Absolutely not.'

With considerable elbow action I manage, after a couple of failed attempts, to shift my carcass onto my good side. That places me in relative close proximity to the couch. Using my arms I rise up on my one good knee and land myself gracelessly onto the couch. And there you have it, Sebastian Synard sitting pretty. I'm affording myself a smile.

'One problem, Mr. Synard. Your crutches are on the other side of the room.'

'They are indeed. Look at that.'

'Remember, at this stage of recovery, your crutches are your salvation. Without them you are in a predicament.'

'Screwed, so to speak.'

She chooses to ignore my turn of phrase. 'Remember— never more than an arm's length away.'

'Never.'

She checks her watch and announces she has to be off. Another appointment. Should I be so lucky.

'I'll leave you with the three Ss.'

'Please do.'

'Slow.' Suitable pause. 'Steady.' Suitable pause. 'Safe.'

'So simple.'

'Exactly so.' She stands up. 'I shall see you tomorrow, same time.' She's off then, front door closed behind her.

Might I add *sad*. Categorically and unreservedly *sad*.

7

I LIKE TO think of myself as pro-active. By noon each day I'm in what I figure will be my standard outfit for the coming weeks—sweat pants, baggy t-shirt, sandals. Relatively easy to climb into, breathable, healing-friendly. There will be no shirking the exercises. No grumbling. No griping. Life will go on, edging closer to normal with each day that passes.

The major decision forcing its way through the curse of recovery is what to do about the upcoming sessions of *On the Rock(s)*. There's another due to start in ten days. It's fully booked. And six more after that in various stages of planning, going into late September.

The doc says at least six weeks before I can expect to drop the crutches for a cane. Maybe twelve weeks to walking unassisted. Up to a year to fully functioning.

So it looked at first like this season of guided tours is shot. Which sucks, since I was just getting things off the ground.

Unless I can hire someone to take my place. I figure once I start using a cane I can do the sitting in restaurants, the eating and drinking. I'm sure I can. I spend an hour coming up with the names of potential fill-ins. The list amounts to three guys from my teaching days who have since retired, the standard way. Two I haven't seen in years and they could be topping up their pensions working at Home Depot now for all I know. The other is someone I ran into a month ago who teaches history as a sessional at the university, who might be able to work it around his schedule, who would likely be good at it, but who I don't like much. A bit of a blowhard.

Not too promising. But then a fourth name jumps onto the list. It suddenly occurs to me that Jeremy might just be willing do it. He had a breakdown after Devlin's death and managed to get extended sick leave from his marketing job at the Department of Tourism. He'd be perfect, if he's up for it. If the pressure isn't too much for him. In fact it might be a good transition back to a normal working life.

I feel hopeful. Which is good. I'll give him a call this evening.

Olsen has called twice, early this morning. I screened both of them. I wanted to think through what I'm going to say to him. I finally call back. He wants to talk on the phone and I don't, and, when I push it, he agrees to come by the house at 1:30. I don't tell him who might show up a half hour later.

This is a hell of a puzzle. As bizarre as it might sound, there is something about Ivo that makes me believe him. Why show up pleading innocent? Why drag his girlfriend into this? Why go back to Latvia to be a chef when he's got no training?

'Because he's off his head and for some insane reason he sees you as his only hope. Because his girlfriend is just as big a weirdo and is probably on drugs just like he is. And because he's taking you for a sucker if you believe anyone would give up Canada for Latvia.'

Olsen is not short on answers. Whether I buy them is another question.

'Sebastian, be reasonable. The guy is a con artist. He probably started training for it in diapers. He only says he wasn't going to kill you because you preempted any possibility of it by jumping. Suddenly he gets it in his head that there's a chance you might not even press assault charges, if he can get you to believe him. He knows for sure his whereabouts are going to be found out at some point. So he turns himself in, having suckered you into believing him, *intent to kill* is dropped, and he gets off with a lighter charge or no charge at all.'

'He's key to the Lester murder.'

'We have yet to establish it was murder.'

'If he does turn himself in, isn't he a more credible witness?'

'That I would agree with. Although, according to what he said to you, he didn't actually see anyone push Lester over the cliff.'

'But he was hired to kill me. Whether he did it or not.' That suddenly sounds incredibly lame.

'His word against theirs.'

'In that case, what's the reason for Ivo being there?'

'How about he showed up unexpectedly and threatened to kill you unless they forked over more money. Ransom money. Of a sort.'

'They didn't do that. I was there. I saw what went on. I saw them team up with Ivo.'

'Your word against theirs. And remember you jumped. Nobody pushed you.'

'What about the money Ivo sent to his mother in Latvia? Where did that come from? And the yellow van? There's a story behind that.'

We're going around in circles. Unless Ivo shows up and the RNC puts the questions to him and they are able to poke holes in his story.

Which is starting to look increasingly unlikely. It's already 2:45. I offer Olsen a Scotch.

Not while he's on duty. To kill time he has a gander at my beverage cabinet. 'I see you lean towards the peaty. I find the smoke tends to overwhelm the more subtle characteristics. I'm more on the light side myself. Auchentoshan. Glenkinchie when I can get it.'

You can tell a lot about a man by his dram. What Olsen drinks certainly won't put any hairs on his chest, to say less than what's in my mind.

The doorbell rings. Olsen looks surprised, whether he is or not. He sits and waits for me to hobble over and answer it.

'Sorry we're late. The Metrobus schedule was way off.' That's very plausible in this city.

The pair sits together on the couch, holding hands, nervous. Ashley is wisely wearing jeans, and a discreet top. It's good to know she has both. Ivo looks less road-weary than he did in the middle of the night. Removed from his head and sitting in his lap is his baseball cap. *Heaven is where all chefs are Latvian*. A bit overt.

Olsen is, as expected, reserved, matter-of-fact, unsmiling. He offers up his name and police rank, but no more.

'Could I have your surname, Ivo?'

'Ozols.' He spells it. Sounds authentic enough to me.

'And Ashley is it?'

'Abbott.' Double *B*. Double *T*. My friends all call me Ash.' The latter point falls quickly to the wayside.

'Do you want to make a statement to the police, Mr. Ozols?'

Yes, he is. He's off to a slow start, but it all comes out in time. That he had encountered Aiden McVickers in a downtown bar on the day before the Signal Hill episode and McVickers had hired him for a strange but simple job that paid very well. They came to an agreement and the next morning he waited near the Battery entrance of the North Head Trail until he received a call on his cellphone. He ran onto the trail, shot past close to the guy just as he was described, continued to the end of the trail and ran home. Later that day Ashley picked up the money in an envelope in her name at the front desk of the Delta as he and McVickers had agreed.

Later McVickers reconnected with him with a second job. Same deal. Bumped into the lady on the Quidi Vidi Trail, knocked her lightly and she fell into the bushes. He ran home. Ashley collected another envelope.

Ivo figured that was it. Then a couple of days later, he's still in bed when he gets a frantic call from McVickers. Can he come up with a van? Maybe. Yes. He thinks so. More complicated than that. Huge money this time. Comes down to murder this time. McVickers wants him to toss a guy over a cliff. It freaks Ivo out, but the thought of all that money is driving him crazy. He convinces McVickers to give him five minutes to think it over. McVickers ups the money.

Ivo talks it over with Ashley and they come up with a plan. He'll get half the money up front and then when it comes to the guy at the edge of the cliff Ivo will refuse to do it, then race off back to Maddox Cove and bugger off in the van with the cash. Ivo phones McVickers. McVickers says a quarter. Ivo agrees and is still shitbaked. The scheme unfolds, just like before. Ivo waits at the end of the trail, this time in a yellow van. Finally he gets the call from McVickers. Gets the money, gets the keys. Drags the victim towards the cliff.

'And then Mr. Synard jumps,' says Ivo. 'I couldn't believe it. I thought, what the hell has he done! The guy's killed himself for no reason. I thought, if there ever was suicide, that was suicide.'

Thanks, Ivo. I'll keep you in mind every day it takes me to fully recover.

Olsen has listened, but not taken any notes.

'And what's your reason, Mr. Ozols, for telling me all this.'

'I was just out to make a few dollars, Inspector Olsen. I had no idea what I was getting into.'

'Mr. Lester is dead. You know that of course.'

'Yes sir, I heard it on the radio the evening after it happened. I figured it had to be him. But it wasn't me who did it. I didn't kill him.'

'You were an accessory, Mr. Ozols.'

'I didn't know I would be. McVickers didn't pay me to do anything but run on the trail. To run close to Mr. Lester, but not to run into him, not to push him over the edge.'

'Didn't you think it was odd, to pay you a pile of money to do that?'

'Maybe. But I needed the money.'

'And the same with the other two jobs—you needed the money?'

'Yes, sir. You see I want to be a chef, sir, in Latvia.'

'I heard.' For Ivo there's a hopeful pause. 'I want you down at the police station. The police have more questions we want answered.' Olsen turns to me. 'While Mr. Synard decides whether he is going to press assault charges.'

'Yes, sir,' says Ivo.

'Ivo wouldn't have killed anyone,' Ashley says. 'He wouldn't be my boyfriend if I thought that.'

That goes down real big with Olsen.

I catch her eye. 'Why is he your boyfriend?'

She looks at Ivo. 'Go ahead,' he tells her.

'I guess you fellows don't follow local hockey. Two years ago Ivo played a few games with the IceCaps. That's how he came to be in St. John's. We met and fell in love. Then he got hit hard and had a real bad concussion and no AHL team wanted to take a chance on him anymore. That was the end of his hockey career. And now all the money's run out.'

'You must have jobs.'

'I do shift work at the food court in the mall. And Ivo works part time at a restaurant downtown, but it's not enough.'

'Not enough,' says Ivo, 'to go home to Latvia and start over.'

I guess not.

I guess I won't be pressing assault charges.

I do think about it a lot. Washed-up hockey players are sad. Can I honestly get in the way of the kid getting a fresh start? Even if he might not make it as a chef? I don't know. And if it wasn't Ivo who roughed me up, it would have been someone else they hired. And it might have been worse. Maybe I wouldn't have had the chance to jump over the cliff. Maybe I really would be dead. Maybe I should count my lucky stars.

The people I want to see swing for this are thousands of kilometres away. The infamous five have all gone back home and life dances on as if nothing has happened. When my rehab exercises are the most excruciating I lie back on the floor and imagine them marching single file up Gibbet Hill, white bags over each head, awaiting the noose. On my good days, I just picture them on the docket at the courthouse, taking the stand in their own defense, only to face wily, calculated cross-examination that extracts body-wracking sobs, prelude to explosive confession.

My recovery days turn to routine. I called Jeremy and managed to talk him into filling in for me on the next tour, and any subsequent ones until I'm back to handling them myself. He'll be great. I've run it by each of the participants, and to a person they have stuck with the tour. Likely it helped that I detailed the nail and screw job that was inflicted on me. I decided to forgo mentioning *how* I came to have the bone broken.

There are small joys to be found in recovery. Nick has turned himself into my right-hand man, catering to me, as they say, hand and foot. Mostly foot. It takes a couple of weeks before I can put any amount of weight on my foot, and successfully work through the pain. His mother has given her permission for Nick to spend every weekend with me, and to come by twice a day during the week, at lunchtime, and after school for an hour. Once summer holidays start I expect to see him even more.

Gaffer is back in my life. Samantha offered to keep the mutt at her place until I was off crutches and able to take him for walks, but I insisted he return to his rightful abode. I need the company. Nick walks him twice a day, and more on weekends. Otherwise, if he needs to do his business, I let him out into the backyard, turd-filled as it gets at times. I give Nick extra game time if he cleans it up on weekends.

It is all-around livable.

Gaffer still fails to see the logic of me lying on the floor pressing, bending, and lifting my legs, all the time counting out the repetitions. His face-licking breaks the monotony, as does the crotch sniffing. I use the latter as a gauge for when I need to go through the torture of taking a shower. Some parts of me are no longer reachable, although daily millimetre increments do add up. The good bathroom news is I no longer have the need to hover. I feel the joy.

Good news as well on the food front. Friends and neighbours have been generous. I had thought the casserole as a culinary concept had died out long ago, but not so.

One evening, about ten days after I arrived home, an unexpected knock comes on the door. I open it to find Ivo and Ashley standing there with a gift bag, a rather heavy one.

'We hope you like it,' says Ashley. 'It's one of Ivo's specialties.'

They don't want to come in because, I assume, they have no idea what kind of relationship we have now.

'In Latvia we call it *sklandrausis*,' says Ivo. 'It will help you get better. We just want to say thank you.'

Sklandrausis turns out to be, as far as I can tell, potato and carrot pie in a rye crust, topped with sour cream sprinkled with cinnamon. He's made several of them—small, individual meal-size pies, one to zap now and the rest to freeze for later. Should I eat something made by a guy who I once thought was out to kill me? Of course. Actually they're not bad. They wouldn't rock the foodies, but they're not bad.

My inability to maneuver about the kitchen with any confidence has given Nick and me a focus. I'm teaching him to cook. Bonding by necessity.

Our aim is one killer dish a weekend. I'm figuring we'll start with soup. Nothing too complicated. Something Thai maybe.

'I'm cool with Thai.'

I retrieve a couple of cookbooks. We look through the pictures and land on a few possibilities. He likes the sound of Tom Yum Kung. Likes saying it over and over and doing a different martial-arts pose for each word.

'It's hot and sour, sweet and salty, all at the same time.'

'Very cool.'

The list of ingredients includes lemongrass, lime leaves, red chillies, and coriander. Not something a kid is used to picking up in the supermarket.

'I have faith in you, pal.' We call up images on the Internet to help him recognize what's on the list.

When he gets to Sobey's he sends me a picture from the produce aisle, then phones. 'Is that coriander?'

'Looks like Italian parsley to me. Anything next to it?'

'Something called cil-an-tro.'

'Buy it.'

You don't learn these life skills playing video games. Or watching crap TV. I want a kid who will go through life knowing that he's self-sufficient, no matter who he ends up with. Or without. I want a kid who can make a damn good soup from scratch.

He does it all—from shelling the shrimp to pounding the lemongrass stalks to making sure it all simmers, not boils—while I'm installed at the kitchen table, supervising. Gaffer sits next to my good foot, sniffing the air.

'Not bad, eh?' Nick says, when we're sitting across the table from each other, soup bowl to soup bowl. Bread sticks on the side.

High five. Heart swollen. Happy as hell to be alive.

It's Monday morning and I'm mid-exercise on the living room carpet when the doorbell rings. It sets off Gaffer, who makes for the door, barking like some little demon guard dog.

'Just a minute!' My voice is poor competition. I'm thinking mailman, a book I ordered on-line. Or a neighbour, another casserole. By the time I am able to resurrect myself, install the crutches, and hobble to the door, I'm expecting whoever it is to be long gone.

I open the door and find Olsen. Gaffer recognizes his scent and starts jumping at his leg for attention.

'Gaffer, settle down.' I get to play the enforcer while Olsen does the playful ear-scratch thing that dogs love. The inspector gives the impression that he and Gaffer were best buds for the few days the dog spent at Samantha's. I'm thinking not. I'm thinking dogs are more discriminating than we give them credit for. Gaffer eventually takes to the couch and settles in next to me, his head resting on his forepaws, staring across the room at Olsen.

The good Inspector hasn't come to chit-chat. There's police business on his mind and he gets straight to it. 'I'll start with Ivo.' Then he momentarily steps aside. 'Normally I wouldn't be discussing a police investigation outside the office. It's purely because it might trigger something that will be of help to us.'

'And I had it put down to generosity. I guess I was being overly optimistic.'

He fails to see the humour. So I detect frustration at the progress in the case?

'Ivo proved useful,' he admits.

'So you believe him?'

'We'll see where it takes us. If he stops cooperating we might not be so sympathetic.'

'Or generous.' A second dirty look. I should know better.

'Did you enjoy the care package?'

It takes a moment before it registers.

'We're keeping an eye on him.'

'You never know what lurks outside your front door.'

'You'd be surprised.'

'In that case I'll avoid the escort service in future. The one that specializes in the infirmed. They don't call it laid-up for nothing.'

Now he smiles. The prick.

Which pushes me past being the nice guy any longer. 'Ivo was hired to kill me. You have the star witness. When are you going to bring back the others to face the music? What are you waiting for?'

'You really think a jury would buy everything he says? The defense lawyer would shoot so many holes through him he'd look like a fucking piece of Swiss cheese.'

Is this policeman lingo? Sounds way too cliché to me.

'We're working other angles. Lester's wife is finally back in Canada. She reported her passport stolen and had to apply for another one from the Canadian Embassy in Paris. It took a while. She arrived back in Toronto two days ago. Lester's ashes were interred yesterday.'

'What was that all about? The stolen passport. And why the hell did Renée try to get her hands on it?'

'We're getting someone from the OPP to question Mira. We figured we'd give her time to get her husband in the ground. Depending on what she has to say, I might fly to Toronto and question her myself.'

'What about McVickers? He's the one who hired Ivo.'

'According to Ivo.'

'Fuck, we both know it was according to Ivo. Stretch your imagination for once and consider he might be telling the truth. Why McVickers?'

'Because he's the only male. Because he looks like he can be trusted? Who knows?'

'Maybe because Lester screwed him and his wife out of more money than the rest of them. Maybe because he had double the reason to be pissed off at the guy.'

'Maybe.'

Maybe. Olsen is really lighting up the investigative neurons with that one.

'And what about Lois, with or without the Ann?'

'No luck finding anything new in Red Deer. That's one thing we'll be trying to get out of Mira. What's the connection?'

'Why did Lois conveniently get herself knocked out of the picture until it was time to go home? And what about the Tennessee wonder woman? Cane one minute, no cane the next.'

'We know all this! What the hell do you think we're doing if not trying to get the pieces to fall in place? Let the police handle it. We fucking know what we're doing.'

'Then why are you talking to me?'

Wrong thing to have said. Olsen stands up to leave.

'Don't count on hearing from me again anytime soon.'

'I'm the one who almost got killed remember!'

'I'm sure you won't let me forget it.'

Gaffer is barking madly at the closed front door. 'You tell him, Gaffer. You never did like him. You never did.'

I got all this time on the sidelines, feeling like a lump and a half. Double-overdosed on Netflix and junk food. Eyes strained out of their sockets from reading when I'm too lazy to get up and adjust the lamp. I soon have to make a start on the whisky blog. With the Scallywag down the drain there was no reason to drag it out. As luck had it, I had jotted down some tasting notes when I cracked open the bottle.

The Thin Man put me in the mood for some armchair sleuthing. So blame it all on Dashiell Hammett.

I decide to start with Lula Jones. Ivo figures she is the most likely person to have done the job on Lester.

What else could I find out about her? What was her connection to Lester? First I need to find out if there really is a Lula Jones in Jonesborough. She hadn't included a phone number on her client profile. And of course she could have an unlisted number or not have a landline. Nevertheless, if I contact every Jones listed in Jonesborough's Internet white pages, I should find someone who has heard of her.

No Jones with the name of Lula or Tallulah, but there are roughly one hundred people listed with the surname Jones. So I start calling. It takes me two days. In some cases it takes several tries, but I do finally reach them all. Fortunately my long-distance package covers the whole of North America.

My line runs: 'Hello, I'm calling from the Federal Bureau of Investigation on an urgent matter. I'm trying to reach a Lula Jones, approximately 80 years old who recently travelled to Newfoundland, Canada. Are you, or do you know of, a woman by the name of Lula Jones? Or by the name of Tallulah Jones.' I sound pleasant, but official. Roughly 75 answer 'No, sir,' or variations thereof. About a dozen 'Let me think, I did know a Lola Jones' (or Lila, or Layla, but never a Lula). Several 'I wish I did. God bless America.' And one 'Do I win anything if I answer correctly?'

All in all, zilch. Which leads to the conclusion she lied, about where she was from at least.

Or she lied about her name. Or lives under an assumed name. Yet if she does live in the U.S. she had to have a passport to fly to Canada, and presumably the RNC checked her passport when they questioned her at the airport. It must have said Tallulah or Lula Jones. And checked her ticket that she was flying to the States.

There are dozens of Tallulah and Lula Joneses in other parts of Tennessee and plenty more throughout the U. S. of A., and plugging in both names to do a Google image search, leads nowhere, except a few places my hormones don't want to be going given my physical limitations.

This seems to be sending me up the veritable creek paddleless when I try Googling the names with extra search terms: pseudonym, a.k.a., stage name, even screen name. Maybe, just maybe, she has a public life under another name.

First screen, nothing. The second, third, and fourth screens, nothing. Then Bingo! A site referencing an article in the *Clayton News Daily* of *Jonesboro*, Georgia, that noted a certain Beckie Barnes (of the Starry Night Hair Salon), a.k.a.

Tallulah Jones, aspiring actress chosen for a part in the movie *Smokey and the Bandit*, several scenes of which will be shot 'right here is good old Jonesboro.' *Smokey and the Bandit*. Burt Reynolds and Sally Field. I remember being glued to it as a kid, before I had taste.

The movie was made in 1977, which would have made Lula/Tallulah in her early 40s. Sure enough, Hollywood comes to town and beautician Beckie Barnes probably lands a two-bit walk on, but has big aspirations, so big she decides to change her name to something more glamourous. I run Tallulah and Lula Jones through a couple of movie sites and it looks like Smokey was her one and only film gig. The *Clayton News Daily* does reveal that she acted in some dynamite local theatre productions over the years, including once as Blanche in A Streetcar named Desire. I can't quite imagine it.

No trouble downloading the movie free from the Internet. Cheesy 1970s blockbuster. Gawd, it's hard going, but there she is, for all of ten seconds, on the streets of Texarkana (a.k.a. Jonesboro), our Lula Jones, looking forty years younger, but definitely Lula.

So. Officially and legally she became Tallulah Jones. But reality inflicted its pain on her star gazing, and my guess is she found herself back at the beauty salon as plain old Beckie Barnes, as everyone in town knew her.

What I need is to get my hands on the list of people who lost money in Lester's Ponzi scheme. Which means contacting Olsen. Like I'd rather commit hari-kari.

Instead, why not go straight to the horse's mouth—the Ontario Securities Commission—and try my luck? I can sound as convincing as the next guy. Besides I feel the need to ramp up my PI skills.

The conversations go better than expected. After four re-routings in the Inquiries department I get to someone who should have an answer to my question.

'I understand that several years ago the OSC heard a case regarding a Mr. Graham Campbell of Toronto. I also understand that one of the clients Mr. Campbell is said to have defrauded is a Rebecca Barnes of Jonesboro, Georgia. Is the OSC able to confirm that Ms. Barnes was indeed one of Mr. Campbell's clients?'

'May I ask who is calling and why you would need this information?'

'My name is Sebastian and I'm a researcher with the CBC-TV's investigative news program *The Fifth Estate*. Perhaps you've heard of it.'

That jolts the energy level at the other end by several notches.

'Yes, I have.'

'Is the list of clients who made representation against Mr. Campbell available to the public, or do I need to make a request through the Freedom of Information and Protection of Privacy Act?'

A definite ramping up.

'Do you mind if I put you on hold for a few moments?'

'Certainly not.'

I can hear the scurry of consultations even though what I'm actually hearing is instrumental music that reeks of a 1990s elevator. I remain patient and professional, however.

'Yes, Mr.... I'm sorry I didn't get your last name?'

'Synard. C-I-N-A-R-D.

'Thank you.'

'And I have yours I believe. Yes, here it is in my notes.'

'You will be pleased to know that summaries of all the Commission's decisions, which would include the names of the parties involved, are available free to the public on our website. I suggest you proceed to the section titled Orders,

Rulings, and Decisions. Then type in the year. The decisions are listed in alphabetical order.'

He's kidding me.

'Should you require further information, Mr. S-Y-N-A-R-D, please don't hesitate to get in touch. And good luck with your research. I hope *The Fifth Estate* is pleased with your level of investigative skill and your understanding of technology.'

The smug little bugger.

He's right. It's all there. *Graham Campbell Investment Management Inc. et al.—Decision.*

And there, in on-screen black and white, is the list of clients who together made application to the OSC for a decision regarding activities of the investment firm of the now dead and buried Graham Lester.

And fourth on the list is one Rebecca Barnes. Just as I suspected.

Life can be very sweet, even if all you can move comfortably is your brain.

That puts Lois and Lula in the pot. And leaves three others—the couple McVickers and Renée—standing on the lip, unaware that I am about to give them an investigative nudge.

First the McVickers. Two for the price of one, if I can find a link. There are no names remotely similar to McVickers, which leads me to think there might be a third-party connection, perhaps a married daughter, or a grandchild, someone close to them who made the bogus investment, or maybe even someone to whom they gave money, that was then invested and lost. With luck, someone who also lives in London, Ontario.

A check of the London white pages gives me a phone number, but also an address. I run each of the names on the list through the same London white pages and a couple of

databases of cellphone numbers and come up with three names
that match. A Ramona Williams and two guys named James,
one with the surname Myers, the other Lam. Could one of
three be among the investors? If so, which one is most likely?
One is female so that's the most promising. But if it was
indeed a grandchild, either one of the other two could be it.
James Myers. James Lam. Don't want to sound ethnically bias,
but I'm thinking Myers more likely than Lam.

I'm getting off on this sleuthing business. The accompany-
ing Scotch is going down nicely, thank you very much Mr.
Inquiries Jerk of the OSC, sitting at your desk, wishing your
day was over, which it is not going to be for several hours, at
which time you have a long commute to some ungodly suburb
and only then will you have a drink in your hand which won't
be half as good as the one I have in mine.

The revenge is sweet. I pour myself another Laphroaig 18.

The next order of business is to take the three names, pump
in each of their addresses on Google Maps and generate a route
map between the address and that of the McVickers. I print
of a copy of each and compare. Williams is the closest. Myers
next. Lam lives in the downtown core of the city. Another
good reason to think he is the least likely. The McVickers are
definitely not centre-of-the city types, and the apple never falls
far from the tree.

I read up on how to disable caller-ID. This time my line is:
'Hello, my name is Malcolm Smith. I'm a friend of Aiden
and Maude McVickers. I wish to speak with [*insert name*]. I
understand that [*insert name*] is a friend or relation of the
McVickers.'

Results not good.

Ramona Williams: 'I don't think so. But then again my
memory is not as good as it used to be. Even with my hearing
aids. Perhaps I met them at seniors' bridge.'

James Myers: 'Sorry, pal, you got the wrong guy. Have a nice day.' Click.

James Lam (third attempt): 'I usually don't answer blocked numbers, but you're persistent. McVickers? Afraid not. If I were you I'd re-enable caller ID. It makes people suspicious.'

What now? All the next day I'm thinking through possibilities. My frustration shows and Nick picks up on that. It's Friday, the start of the weekend.

'Maybe I can help.'

I'm not sure I should be getting into the details of what I'm up to. And I can't see how he can be of much help. But, he bugs me enough that I let him in on the bare bones version.

'Let me try Facebook?'

Facebook I have no intention of ever joining. I can't think of anything worse than a holy load of former students wanting to be friends with me. The less anybody knows of my life as an ex-teacher the better.

Two hours later, and a lot of boring pictures of badly dressed people with their dogs, cats, or grandchildren, Nick strikes gold!

'Whaddya think, a possibility?'

There are hundreds of Nathan Smiths, but not so many Nathan A. Smiths, and the profile picture of this one, geared up for work in the Alberta Tar Sands, hits me where it counts. Even with the hardhat he's the spit of Aiden.

'Look at that,' says Nick, 'he graduated high school in London, Ontario.'

'Sweet!'

And almost at the end of an endless reel of monster-size trucks and hyperactive females at backyard barbecues up comes a family shot, and there they are bright as the Christmas lights behind them, Aiden and Maude and Nathan A.

'Sweet! Nicholas, man, you're a bona fide little genius!'

'Does that mean we can order take-out from India Gate?'

'You, my friend, can eat rogan josh until the sacred cows come home.'

'Yes!'

That leaves Renée. Dear, dear misguided Renée. Who I had such high hopes for until her true, post-coital self emerged. I'm thinking she's going to be the toughest nut to crack. After what her pill-dropping did to Nick, crack her I will.

I suspect her name is for real. My latest bout with the Internet tells me there are plenty of Sipp winegrowers in Alsace. Renée's name doesn't pop up, but that wouldn't mean much other than the fact that as the hot-tempered ex-wife she's been expunged from anything and everything to do with the winery. Renée's no more in the vineyards, and now doing God knows what. Being severely pissed off by the loss of her divorce money, among other things. Money that someone else, for some reason, invested. I spend a lot of time trying to find a French connection with any of the names on the investor list. Nothing other than a few photos of a double-balding, overweight and badly dressed pair of brothers on a Seine river cruise.

The key to outing Renée has to be Mira, Lester's wife. Renée didn't steal Mira's passport without good reason. The two had to be up to no good, together. Which means, if Olsen's theory about Lois Ann and Mira holds water, the three of them were all working together. And when I go back to my records, Lois Ann was the first to sign up for the tour, followed by Lester, then Renée. While Mira jets off to France.

Lester arranges to have her passport stolen, so he can spend more time getting his rocks off with Lois Ann after the tour. Only the rocks he gets off on are not the ones he planned on.

Bad pun. But it's getting late, and time to call it a night. Before which Gaffer needs to go out the back door for his final business trip of the day. He's exceptional for getting straight to the task at hand and heading back in the house when it is completed. Mid-business tonight, though, he's suddenly distracted. He cuts things short and jumps into his demon dog routine, barking like mad at something outside the fence. From where I am on the deck, peering through the dark, trying to see what it could be, proves useless. A cat most likely, or another dog. Eventually Gaffer's barking subsides, and he continues where he left off.

He joins me on the deck because he knows dogs who do their business when prompted are good dogs and deserving of a treat. He also knows that sitting by my feet and waiting patiently, even though his barking has impacted negatively on his reputation, might result in a chow-chow (as it is known to the two of us), his all-time favourite treat—organic sweet potato and bison biscuits, grain-free, gluten-free, and with just the right amount of crunch. Gaffer is a true foodie among dogs. He hasn't yet acquired a taste for Scotch, but that may come.

8

I WAKE UP knowing I desperately need something to firmly link Renée to Mira. Since getting out of bed and upright requires a great deal of effort still, I make the choice of lying there while the thought patterns align themselves, Gaffer with his head resting on my good leg.

It would be useful to know when exactly Mira arrived in Paris. The bit of information is as close as a phone call to Olsen, having him check the customs stamp on her passport. I decline.

Let's assume that after her divorce Renée moved away from Riquewihr, if indeed she ever did live there. To where? I'm thinking Paris, considering the way she was talking about it. I'm thinking she moved to Paris to start over. Her friend Mira (whom she met wherever, when they were students, on some cruise, who knows) comes to visit. A whole scenario starts filling my head. I should lie in bed more often.

They get talking about husbands. And money. How they have no use for the first and plenty of uses for the second. How Mira and her sister Lois have this plan cooked up to get rid of Lester. Lois who lost a half million to Lester's scheme, but who got it back since she's the sister-in-law he always liked. Liked so much in fact that she is able to lure him on this tour in Newfoundland. And where he'll have an *accident*.

What do you think, Renée, will you come in on it? We need four more people to fill the tour quickly. Lois is working on people she met at the Securities Commission hearing, people who were especially bitter. She thinks this couple from London are game. They lost a pile of money they had set aside for their grandson. And a woman from somewhere near Atlanta. A bit of an actress. Lost all her life's savings and she's so old she's got nothing more to lose. Once Graham is out of the picture, the entire estate comes to me. I pay off the others and the three of us—me and you and Lois—ride off into the sunset.

Très, très bon, says Renée who I'm thinking now wasn't one of the investors, but would like a generous boost to her bank account. Living in Paris isn't cheap, and the divorce settlement is dwindling fast.

I have all this figured out and I'm still not out of bed.

The rest of the morning is anti-climactic. True, in the physical sense, there are advances—less crutch support, more use of the game leg, increased mobility on the stairs—but they can't keep up with the mind's feverish drive to crack the case wide open.

It's sunny outside and, to judge by the t-shirts passing along the street, warm to boot. When summer finally arrives in Newfoundland it is a much-talked-about, blessed event. I decide this is the day I'll venture as far as the coffee shop at the end of my street. My first self-propelled adventure into the great outdoors.

Off I jaunt and suddenly I'm feeling very good about being alive, my virility boosted. Slowly down my few front steps, hippy-hop maybe a hundred metres along the sidewalk, and

I'm in luck. There's a nifty vacant table outside, perfect for a lone occupant who needs room for a less-than-flexible limb. It's preferable to negotiating the door to the inside. That will be an exercise in virility for another day.

I descend to the sitting position without embarrassment, leaving me thinking, yes, next week I start regular visits to a physio centre, and give me a couple more weeks and I'll be transitioning to a cane, and won't that be swell.

The staff of Coffee Matters is all over me, given that I've been a regular customer since I moved onto the street. They know about my near-death experience, and are happy to note the evidence hasn't completely faded from my face. Pity gives way to jocular sympathy. The caffè latte and mint-chocolate granola square are on the house.

Sitting in the sun, sipping my latte, reading Dashiell Hammett, watching the procession of pedestrians, it's all a normalizing experience. To the extent that it can be, given the exposed female attributes that pass me by. I try not to dwell on them. The flesh is willing, the surrounding area uncommonly weak. Obligatory celibacy has few merits.

By early afternoon, back at the house, I finish up *The Thin Man* and begin writing up the newest blog entry for *Distill My Reading Heart!* I post on the same day each month. It keeps me disciplined.

The blog entry always starts with a picture of the whisky, and luckily I took a shot of Scallywag when I first decided it was the chosen one. My impressions of the dram are still fresh, and together with some info on the producer, Google-gleaned and from several of my whisky books, it makes for an entertaining few paragraphs. I keep it light and interject the odd clever turn of phrase. Whisky lovers like a drinking buddy with a sense of humour. It eases the guilt of an expensive bottle.

My non-drinking buddy Gaffer has to content himself with lying next to me, occasionally resting his chin on the edge of my laptop in support when he notices I'm struggling with a particular sentence. I feel sorry for him. He's wondering what has happened to the guy who played chase and used to be so much fun. I try to reassure him it will return in time, and slip him the occasional chow-chow to ease the boredom.

It seems he anticipates Nick's daily arrivals with a time-keeper's precision. He becomes that much more alert as the time approaches, and at the first touch of Nick's foot on the front step Gaffer is off like a shot to meet him. The pair are inseparable and I never tire of watching them rolling over the carpet, Nick's head buried in Gaffer's fur. Gaffer may be costing more than I was counting on, but there's no price tag on a boy's love for his mutt, even when the mutt smells.

After Nick returns from the dog walk, he piles Gaffer into the tub and gives him a thorough soaping. From downstairs I can tell it's turned into something of a game. Gaffer eventually emerges the winner and comes racing down the stairs, soapless, but thoroughly wet. He stands in the middle of the kitchen floor and shakes himself repeatedly, a swath of water whipping across my legs.

I could get mad but I hold back. In the last few days I have learned that there are things worth getting upset about, and then there are others in the great scheme that mean nothing.

When Nick leaves for his other home, I dish out some food for Gaffer to take his mind off it, make a sandwich for myself, then settle back into the blog. I'm a couple of hours late with the new posting. I usually try to have it online for readers getting home from work and settling into their winding-down dram.

I'm ready to plunge ahead with the second half of the piece, conscious of striking that balance between upbeat and mellow.

Not so hard to do since I won't review books I don't like.

The Thin Man was Dashiell Hammett's fifth and final novel. It was published in January of 1934, just a month after the repeal of Prohibition in the United States. The country was ready to drink and the novel gave every reason to, if one were to judge by the lifestyle of the chic New York couple at the centre of the story. Scotch arrives on page two and a drink is forever close at hand, any time of the day.

The opening paragraph could be better, but I'll stick with it. I need to move on. Before any smartass quips about the characters and witty kudos about the writing style, there needs to be a short summary of the plot. Time flies when you're working against the clock. Eventually the piece comes together. And looking good, with still an hour to midnight. All it needs is a solid proofread before pressing the *publish* button and the inboxes of my 22 followers across the globe get their monthly injection of *Distill my Reading Heart!*

Gaffer has been patient, but he needs to do his business before calling it a night. That means uprooting myself from the armchair and hanging out on the deck for the several minutes it takes for the mutt to find his own good place and time. The air is surprisingly warm still, with stars in the night sky determined to make themselves visible through the meddlesome city lights. It is at times like this that I wish I still indulged myself with a cigarette. That habit I gave up long ago, although I have moments like this when a deep draw and a cool, lengthy exhale in the near-romantic night air would be a godsend.

It's the stuff of dreams. Dreams die, very quickly!

First one crutch, then the other is cut out from under me. I grab onto the deck railing to keep from falling. When I right myself enough that I can turn to look behind, there they are, the women of my nightmare. Dearest Renée! And her partner in this depravity, whom I have never seen before, but can only be Mira.

It is Mira who jumps me and forces a hard silicone ball into my mouth, with red leather straps on each side that wrap around to the back of my head and buckle so goddamn tightly that I can't make a sound. And which hurt like bloody hell.

Jesus Christ!

I'm an unstable mess. I can't stand, there's nowhere to sit, I'm forced to hang onto the railing or slump to my knees. All the time Gaffer, who I can't see, is barking like mad at the pair of them, until there is a sudden yelp and a wounded whine. That jeesley Renée! There's murder in my veins and nothing I can do with it.

'Inside!' snarls Mira. They hand me back my crutches. 'Or we re-break your bloody leg.'

I'm in a state. What choice do I have but scuff and drag myself past the door. The pair follow, shut the door to the deck and draw the curtain across it. Gaffer is left outside, barking for a short while, until he seems to give up in pain. At least he's alive, although who knows what the fuck they've done to him.

I flop onto the couch, a wretched, gagged piece of crap with an upper left leg feeling like someone had just stomped on it with a pair of cleats.

'You have two choices,' Mira says. 'Either you agree to shut up and we take off the gag, or you act like an idiot and we keep it on. Which is it?'

The gag comes off. I spend the next five minutes working my jaw to try getting it back in enough shape to swear at the bastards when the time is right. In the meantime they do the talking.

'Surprised to see me, *Sébastien*? I'm surprised to be here. I should be on a beach in the south of France instead of having to finish up where we left off.' Renée is in the armchair, helping herself to my Scotch, my fucking favourite eighteen-year old Laphroaig. 'I'd offer you a drink but I'm not sure you would take anything that I'd pour.'

'I'd introduce myself,' says Mira, 'but I have a feeling you already know who I am. By the way, have you still got my passport?'

'Try the cops.'

'Friends of yours? Unfortunately, they won't do you any good, not where you're going.'

'Where's that?' Not that I really want to know.

'Let's just say,' Renée adds eagerly, 'this time you won't have the choice of how you go down.'

'Where the hell is he?' says Mira, checking her phone, for the time, I presume. 'It's not like there's any goddamn traffic in this place.'

Is there any way to confuse the bastards? It's a dumb question.

'You went all the way to France and came back again, just to wish me good-bye?'

'Montréal, actually. There was unfinished business back in Newfoundland.'

'This place does grow on you.'

'You always had a sense of humour, *Sébastien*.'

'Even in bed.'

'You went to bed with him?' barks Mira.

'It got me your passport,' Renée barks back.

'Not for long,' I tell her.

'I underestimated you.'

'You might just do it again.'

'Not this time,' Mira snaps, as if to point out that, had she been the one in charge, things would have gone the way they had been planned. In other words, I'd be dead.

'How was your husband's funeral, Mira? You must have been pleased.'

She smiles at my brazenness, taking it as a challenge. 'Didn't come soon enough.'

Being candid comes with being convinced I'll never have the opportunity to repeat anything she says.

'You'll make good use of his money, you and Renée. And Lois.'

'That's good. That's very good. We're definitely making the right move in getting rid of you.'

'The McVickers and Lula—they were happy enough with their cut?'

'Very.'

'What makes you think I haven't told the cops all I know?'

'You mean Inspector Olsen,' says Renée, 'the one who is screwing around with your ex-wife? The one your kid hates? I don't think you want to be telling him anything.'

So the bitch wasn't in the bedroom with the door closed that night.

'And unfortunately,' chimes in Mira, 'when the time comes that you planned on playing the big hero, you'll have disappeared. Your body never found. Sad, isn't it?'

'The both of you are what's sad! And fuckin stupid if you think you'll get away with it.'

'Too bad you won't be around to see it happen.'

There's a knock on the back door.

'Finally!' says Mira.

She answers it. Who should stroll into the living room but Ivo.

He won't look at me.

'You big bastard!'

'I'm sorry, Mr. Synard.'

And I fucking believe he is.

'If I didn't agree to do it, they were going to blame it all on me. Leave me to take the rap.'

'For fuck's sake,' says Mira, 'it's the money. You want the rest of the goddamn money.'

That I believe.

'What happened, Ivo? You couldn't resist the money? Tell you what, Ivo, you walk out of here and I'll double the money they're paying you. I'll double the money and I'll tell the cops I believe your story that you didn't knock Lester over the cliff. Double the money, Ivo. That'll get you and Ashley a nice little restaurant in Latvia. And enough left over for an apartment, I'd say. Wouldn't you?'

'You shut up!' Mira yells at me.

'And I'll swear in court I believe your story that you didn't plan to push me over the cliff. Because you didn't, did you? You weren't really going to do it, were you?'

'Where's that fucking gag?' Mira shouts at Renée.

Ivo is sweating buckets. 'I wasn't really, Mr. Synard.'

'I believe you. And you don't have to go through with it now. They can't do it without you, Ivo. I bet you're the one who found the cliff where they want me dumped. They don't even know where to go. They don't…'

The ball practically crushes my teeth. Mira yanks the leather straps together even tighter than before. I nod yes to Ivo and keep nodding. Yes, Ivo. Yes, Ivo. You can do it. You can walk out of here and drive away in the van.

Mira's open hand slaps viciously across my face. I manage still to keep my eyes on Ivo.

'We should just kill him now.'

Thanks, Renée. You're an even bigger sweetheart than I thought.

'Don't be an idiot,' Mira barks at her. 'We stick to the damn plan. No evidence in the house. We shut him up for good in the van. Give him his crutches and let's get the hell out of here.'

Ivo hesitates. Good, Ivo. Hesitate some more. You can do it, man. It's all in your hands.

It fires Mira up even more. 'Don't fuck up now, Ivo. You're in over your fuckin head and you know it. We get in the van, we dump the body, we drive to Halifax. In twenty-four hours you and the girlfriend are on a flight to Europe. Got it. That's the plan.'

'We'll triple the money,' pipes up Renée.

'Jesus!' says Mira. Then takes a deep breath. 'Okay, we triple the money. Now give the bastard his crutches and get him in the van.'

Ivo does as he is told. I can't give up on him yet. A lot can happen between here and wherever.

'We'll get him in the van, you tidy up the place,' Mira says to Renée. 'No sign of any struggle.'

There's no point in resisting. There is a point in looking as strong and healthy as I can manage, in looking like a man Ivo wouldn't want to knock off. Who was kind and generous to him. Who ate his sklandrausis for fuck's sake.

A van is backed into the driveway, as far away from the street as possible. Nice black paint job. With the light off over the back door, it's practically invisible.

Six-foot-six Ivo has control of me, while Mira scouts the outside. She opens the driver and front passenger doors, blocking any view from the street, then slides open the side door. Another quick check and she signals Ivo.

I'm not going anywhere very quickly, and at one point Ivo takes away the crutch on my bad side and replaces it with himself, his steel arm under my armpit. He's not being particularly rough, which I think is telling me something. I'd goddamn smile at him if I could.

I'm in the van and seated. Ivo hands the crutches to

Ashley who is silently perched in the seat behind me. Ashley looks to be in shock. My eyes widen into Ivo's as he seatbelts me in. He turns away, but not before I give him a thumbs up. You can do it, man. You can do it—save your own skin and mine, too.

Mira closes the side door. They've thought of everything. The window next to me is covered with an adhesive film that prevents anyone from outside seeing in.

Renée boards the van and takes another of the seats behind me. The house is looking tidy no doubt. It suddenly dawns on me that I haven't laid eyes on Gaffer, or heard him. I'm thinking Ashley did something to shut him up. She's in shock for good reason.

Mira slams the other side door and, once Ivo is behind the steering wheel, she gets in the passenger seat.

Both doors close. 'Okay,' says Mira, 'we're out of here.'

Ivo hesitates.

'What the fuck you waiting for?'

Ivo has yet to turn the key.

Mira rifles through an oversized handbag. Out comes a covered knife. She slides away the plastic sheath and reveals an eight-inch blade. The polished stainless steel of a Jamie Oliver chef's knife, just like the one I got free with the stamps I collected at Sobeys. German steel, ergonomic handle, ending in a murderous point.

'I can do the job now, or I can wait. Your choice. In the meantime, you fuck up and the girlfriend might just go on the chopping block with him.'

Ivo's head turns to her as he starts the van. In the rearview mirror I can see the glare in his eyes. He turns on the headlights.

'Put that thing away, I can't drive with that in my face.'

The van moves ahead and the knife goes back in the sheath,

then back in the handbag.

He pulls onto Military Road, heading west.

He has gone no more than a few dozen metres when two cop cars, red and blue flashing lights suddenly on full glare, come racing down Bannerman Street, then onto Military, swerving in opposite directions, and completely blocking the street.

'Christ!' yells Mira.

Two more cop cars are storming up behind us.

'In there!' yells Mira, hand pointing to the narrow road that leads to Government House, unsuspecting home of Newfoundland's Lieutenant Governor. The van makes a sharp right turn, smashing through the white wooden gate spanning the entrance. The pair behind me are frantic, backlit by the headlights of a cop car tight behind us.

'Where do I go? Where do I go?' Ivo shouts. A security guard bolts from his hut, too late to stop anyone. He jumps back, narrowly escaping being hit by the cop car.

'Out the other fucking end!' Mira's adrenalin is pumping madly. 'Faster, for Christ's sake!'

The road cuts in front of Government House, where two more security guards burst through the front door, onto the pillared entrance, also too late.

I know these grounds. I've walked Gaffer here. The road goes straight through a grove of trees, where it exits through another access point, onto King's Bridge Road. The van barrels towards the exit. Smashing through the gate barring it, only to find the exit road blocked by another pair of cop cars. My appreciation for the RNC has skyrocketed.

Ivo slams on the brakes, swerves to the right and onto the dirt road that goes behind Commissariat House. The cop car behind us is momentarily jilted, but in no time is back on track. By now the van has struck the grounds of St. Thomas'

Church. Swerves right in time to escape hitting a corner of it. Down and around a hairpin curve and on to the lower level parking lot, screeching to a lurching stop because cop cars, lights flashing madly, are blocking the exit onto the street.

It throws me sideways, sending massive pain up the bad leg, freeing the other from behind the driver's seat. Freeing it enough that I can raise it up and ram it with every ounce of energy in me between the two front seats and into Mira's shoulder, sending the bulk of her square onto the dash, her head bouncing off the windshield!

Christ, I'm alive.

Surrounded by cops with their handguns drawn.

I'm sitting by myself on the steps of the oldest church in the city. An excellent example of Early Gothic Revival, as I told the tour group that first day, when we passed it on our way up Signal Hill.

I'm somewhat revived myself. The parking lot is teeming with cops, all looking very efficient. The questionable three-some are distributed in three different cop cars, each giving a statement I assume. The fourth, indisputably the ringleader, on her way to the hospital for examination. My kick took the good out of her. She'll threaten to sue no doubt.

The cop blocking the entrance to the parking lot lets another car in, not one of their own this time. He points the driver in my direction.

Nick reaches me first. He bursts into tears and hugs me fiercely.

'It's okay, pal. I'm fine. You're dad's a tough dude.'

Samantha is not far behind. 'Oh, God, Sebastian, what happened? Were they really going to kill you?'

'The knife definitely had my name on it.'

Now she's crying. And I start to fill up. Which makes for

pretty much of a tear-jerker all around.

Olsen looks on. 'You okay?'

'These guys say you called it in. How the hell did you know something was up?'

'Can I get him now, Mom?' Nick says.

His mother nods and Nick is off like a shot to the car. He opens the door and out jumps Gaffer, half running, half limping towards me. He jumps on me and starts licking my face all over.

'He's the reason. He knew something was wrong,' says Nick. 'He's the one who saved you.'

Once Renée kicked him and shut the door behind her, he couldn't get back in the house. Apparently he found a way out of the backyard and took off for Samantha's house.

'We walked it enough times that he remembered,' says Nick. 'I couldn't believe it and when I saw him limping I knew something was definitely screwy.'

'Plus you hadn't posted to your blog,' says Olsen.

'C'mon.'

'No, really, this is the day every month, you never miss. And it wasn't there.'

Life smacks me in the teeth, and I still got reason to smile. I got to think there'll be others.

9

THE VET BILL sets me back on my ass. Even though young Gaffer is all over the news reports, and the story practically goes viral, the vet clinic still expects its chunk of flesh. The good news is he'll be fine in a few weeks, recovering very well at home on prime rib and sautéed sweet potato. The word has reached me that he's being nominated for a dog hero award. No cash attached unfortunately.

As for the humans in this high drama, they have not come out looking so good. Although Mira recovered nicely from her dislocated shoulder and minor concussion, the answers she provided the RNC didn't match so well with Renée's version of events. Both women are trying to shift the blame onto Ivo, but there's too much that doesn't add up, according to Olsen, who has given me a limited version of their statements.

Ivo still contends he didn't push Lester over the cliff. Whether he would have dumped me on the second opportunity is something I continue to debate. Why I still have sympathy for the guy is something I don't understand.

The RNC has charged Mira with kidnapping and intent to murder, and Renée and Ivo with being accomplices. The

McVickers are being brought back from Ontario and Lois (Ann) from Alberta for further questioning. And, depending on how much Lula is implicated, the RNC will undertake extradition procedures to get her back from the States.

Olsen is being more human than he has been since all this started. He couldn't help but be impressed with what I (and Nick) discovered about Lula and the McVickers on the Internet. It's helping to build the case.

A few days after my latest return from the brink, he comes by the house one evening and we share a few whiskies. It was his idea, and who's willing to say no to a cop.

He brings along an unopened bottle of Scotch. It's something called Octomore, made by Bruichladdich. I know of it, but have never seen a bottle. It's reputed to be the peatiest whisky made.

'A friend of mine picked it up for me in Toronto.'

'I thought you didn't like peat?'

'I bought it for you. But I'm willing to have a go.'

A peace offering. A noble one at that.

'The boys have followed up on Lula and the McVickers. They found out a few more things. Seems Lula was quite an accomplished exponent of martial arts in her day. State champion in her age category a number of years running.'

'Flexible in more ways than one.'

'Maude McVickers, formerly Maude Heffern, was born in Bonavista Bay.'

'You're joking.'

'Moved to Ontario when she was twenty and met Aiden.'

'That's why she ate so much cod! And she didn't swallow *The Dictionary of Newfoundland English* after all.'

'Aiden was into the stock market. Made quite a bit of money. Too bad Lester screwed him out of most of it.'

'He had every reason to despise the guy.'

'Despise is one thing. Helping set him up to be murdered is another.'

Spoken like a true officer of the law. And in this case I agree.

The Octomore is gold to a peathead like myself. Olsen takes a swallow and there's a brief gripping of the teeth.

'Not sure I could learn to like it.'

'More for me in that case.'

We can chuckle.

I wonder out loud what he thinks of Ivo now. Is there any sympathy there at all?

'Ivo fucked up and he knows he fucked up. He wanted the quick bucks too badly.'

Olsen's right. 'Do you really think he would have gone through with it?'

'I could give him the benefit of the doubt on one. But not two.'

'Maybe so.'

'You can never count on how it'll play out with a jury, if it gets that far. One thing's for sure. He'll never get his restaurant in Latvia.'

'That's too bad in a way. If he'd played by the rules and saved his money, over time he might have been able to do it.'

'That's hockey players for you. Big money one minute and, when something goes wrong, zilch the next.'

'Not easy.'

'Sebastian, had Mira knifed you, he would have slung you over some cliff in the dead of night, weighed down with God knows what. The sea lice would be getting fat and nobody would have had a clue what happened to you.'

'I feel sorry for the big fucker, that's all.'

'Your heart is bigger than your brain.'

He can see it doesn't go over too well with me.

'I'll take that as a compliment.' I let him off with it this time. Probably the Octomore is getting to me.

School is out for the summer and I see a lot more of Nick, which suits me just fine. I'm not sure what his mother thinks, but she lets it pass and I'll take whatever comes my way.

Gaffer's limp gradually fades away and on most days he and Nick can be found in Bannerman Park and occasionally across the street on the grounds of Government House. Gaffer is a big hit with the security staff. His reputation has preceded him. One day he and Nick were invited inside to meet the Lieutenant Governor and his wife. Nick came rushing back to me with a selfie to prove it.

I was sitting on the front step, as I often do when the weather is warm. My leg has improved enough that I'm reasonably comfortable. Neighbours come by and we chat, or perfect strangers, because they all know how I twice dodged the bullet. I much preferred being anonymous.

Still, you take what you can get. And when the office miniskirts go by, I'm thinking yes, Synard, your time will come again. With a steel pin in you it could prove that much more exciting.

One day I'm sitting there alone, and walking past on the other side of the street is a couple. He's tall and she comes up to his shoulder. They don't look over, probably because they spied me from a distance, and anyway I'm not certain it's them.

'Ivo.' Loud enough for the fellow to hear, though they've gone past.

They stop and look back and across the street. Ivo raises his hand. I know he's been released on bail. I thought the court would have issued an order that he stay away from me, but it didn't for some reason. I guess some things get forgotten. Or maybe not.

I wave them over. There is a great deal of hesitation, and some serious discussion between them, but eventually they cross the street and stop at a cautious distance.

'How are things?'

I like to keep my edge.

'Ivo lost his job,' says Ashley.

I'm not surprised. The media was all over him, especially once they discovered he had played for the IceCaps.

'I managed to keep mine,' she adds.

'Maybe I'll come up with something,' Ivo says. 'I keep trying.'

Conversation doesn't come easy. They look at each other, then at me, before almost giving up in silence.

'How's the leg?' Ivo says finally.

'Getting there. In a couple of weeks I graduate to a cane.'

'Good.'

'It *is* good, Ivo. It could have been a lot worse, as we both know.'

They're thinking they should move off.

'Ivo, I have a question. Don't feel you have to answer it.'

I doubt he wants me to ask anything that needs such a caveat.

'If Mira had stabbed me that night, would you have dumped the body?'

He thinks about it for a few seconds. 'Probably.'

I guess I don't want to hear anymore. I shrug and look away.

'Mr. Synard, the thing was I wasn't going to let her kill you. You were good to me. I wasn't going to let that happen. That was my carving knife she had. She wanted a knife and I gave it to her. If I had refused to get involved, she would have hired someone else, and you would be dead for sure. This way I thought I could save you.'

They take a last look at me and move on.

They've gone more than a few steps. 'Hey!'

Only Ivo looks back.

'Thanks,' I call out, not loud, but loud enough for him to hear.

He doesn't say anything. He raises his hand slightly before turning away again and walking on.

There's no figuring it all out. The day comes when I walk with a cane and I feel comfortable joining Jeremy and the new crews who've signed up for *On the Rock(s)*. Joining them just for the meals. It is good to be out and about and in the real world again. And there's nothing but goodwill all around. I can provide more than enough entertaining dinner conversation.

For some reason, which I know is odd but which I can't explain, they get off on being part of a tour that now has a certain notoriety. Jeremy tells me he's overheard some of them announce it proudly to the concierge at the Delta. And now, with me showing up for dinner each evening, it's like The Dead Man Cometh.

Several of them suggest I open a Twitter account to keep everyone updated on my recovery and the court proceedings as they unfold. I think not.

'Seriously,' says one guy. 'The tour company could become huge. You could be upping the prices, hiring staff, doing seminars in the off-season. Here's the angle: Miracle Man survives to lead others on a tour of the crime scene. Especially if the bozos get convicted. Even if they don't, and this trial hits the Internet, there'll be no stopping it. Sebastian, you're sitting on a gold mine. I'd be the first to invest if you're looking for backers.'

Mainlanders tend to get carried away. When I go home and collapse in the armchair, Gaffer wedged next to me on the right, a healthy dram of Octomore on the end table to the left, I'm thinking *investors*, that's the last thing I want to have to deal with.

I just want to keep it slow and simple.

The telephone rings.

'Yes.'

'I'd like to speak with Mr. Sebastian Synard.'

'You got him.'

'I'm calling from CBC Television in Toronto. I'm a researcher from a network program called *The Fifth Estate*. Perhaps you've heard of it.'

He's joking. 'I have.'

'We've been following your story. *The Fifth Estate* would like to explore the possibility of doing a twenty-minute segment on what's happened, for broadcast in the fall.'

There is a long pause, of my own making.

'Are you still there, sir.'

'Yes.'

'Of course you don't have to agree to it right away. I should tell you we have an average weekly audience of close to 700,000 viewers. How about you take some time to think about it and I call you back on Monday?'